fragment

fragment

CRAIG RUSSELL

thistledown press

Thistledown Press Ltd.
410 2nd Avenue North
Saskatoon, Saskatchewan, S7K 2C3
www.thistledownpress.com

Library and Archives Canada Cataloguing in Publication

Russell, Craig, 1956, June 18–, author
Fragment / Craig Russell.
Issued in print and electronic formats.
ISBN 978-1-77187-111-2 (paperback). –ISBN 978-1-77187-112-9 (html). –ISBN 978-1-77187-113-6 (pdf)
I. Title.
PS8635.U868F73 2016   C813'.6   C2016-905252-4
C2016-905253-2

Cover and book design by Jackie Forrie
Printed and bound in Canada

Thistledown Press gratefully acknowledges the financial assistance of the Canada Council for the Arts, the Saskatchewan Arts Board, and the Government of Canada for its publishing program.

Acknowledgements

Many thanks to Thistledown Press for their steadfast encouragement and insightful direction in the development of this novel. And there's no question but that I won the lottery when Thistledown Press asked Michael Kenyon to be the editor for *Fragment*. He challenged me to explore the story more deeply with thoughtful questions and suggestions. Michael, it's been a privilege to work with you.

As I wrote the early drafts of this novel four readers, Paul St. Pierre, Margaret Pople, Heather Russell-Smith, and Roger Rigelhof, each at different points in the process and each in their own way, helped renew my belief in the story. Thank you.

For many years Brandon's actors, producers, directors, and stage crew, far too numerous to name, have shared their love of theatre with me. How could I hear what we've done together and not hope to write words worth sharing?

I've had the great good luck to live within a Renaissance family. To be surrounded by the creative energies of our daughter, actor Heather Russell-Smith, our son, musician Ian Russell, and my wife, visual artist Janet Shaw-Russell, has been the greatest inspiration and joy.

Note: The quoted lines on page 109 are from Lord Byron's *Childe Harold's Pilgrimage*.

To Janet, for sharing tears and laughter over the fate of imaginary beings.

Consider the nature of ice.

The heat of fusion is one of its mysteries.

The heat of fusion governs the transmutation from ice to water — that miraculous moment when H_2O changes from solid to liquid.

As you heat ice, its temperature rises.

The formula is easy. Add one calorie of heat to one gram of ice and its temperature goes up one degree. What could be simpler?

But there's a point at which something magical happens.

Just when you reach the temperature where ice melts — thirty-two degrees Fahrenheit for Americans or zero degrees Celsius for the rest of the world — you hit a strange plateau.

You can't just add one more calorie and jump from zero degree ice to plus-one degree liquid water.

No, you must add *eighty* calories of heat before that amazing change takes place.

It takes *eighty* times the energy to make that important transformation occur.

Ice is resilient stuff and it takes a lot of energy to make even a small amount of it melt away.

PART ONE

New York — October 6

"Tonight's satellite feed comes live from Scott Base, on the coast of Antarctica."

The host of *Innovation-TV*, Jay Traljesic, is tall and slim. In his mid-thirties, he has carefully dressed in an open-collared shirt and black jeans; he believes he looks like a young professor. He'd like to make co-eds weak in the knees.

His studio set is an eclectic mix of sharks' teeth, Samurai blades and voodoo dolls, artifacts he's collected from around the globe. Behind him the woman's face, framed by honey-blonde hair and dominated by Nordic blue eyes, fills the giant screen. Her slim shoulders are fluid under a black turtleneck.

"Doctor Kate Sexsmith is a Canadian scientist, an expert on the polar ice caps. Hello, Doctor. Or should I say good morning? It's tomorrow morning where you are, right?"

"Yes, good morning. It's 6:45 AM here." The woman blurs and reappears as she adjusts the webcam that captures her image. "It's October and spring has arrived, so the sun's been up for over an hour."

"Doctor. May I call you Kate?" Jay consults his notepad. "You have news about the Ice Shelf."

"Yes, Jay. I'm a scientist here at New Zealand's Scott Base, near the Ross Sea Ice Shelf."

As with most guests, Jay knows that Dr. Sexsmith will feel obliged to supply some general background before she can get to the point of the interview. On this occasion he doesn't mind listening. She moves back from her camera, revealing an attractive figure, and points to a large wall map.

"This is a polar view of Antarctica." She smiles and points. "Here is the Ross Sea. It's ringed by the teeth of the Trans-Antarctic Mountains, and is a thousand kilometres wide."

She extends her arm with unconscious grace and locates a crumb of land deep inside the bay, near where an expanse of white fills much of the Sea.

"This is our location. Ross Island."

Her hand brushes across the white expanse.

"And just to our south is the Ross Ice Shelf."

"That's what the early explorers called 'The Barrier'?" Jay says.

"With good reason. It's a plate of ice, as big as France, seven-hundred-metres thick, floating on the ocean. Roald Amundsen, the first person to reach both the North and South Poles, called it 'The Imposing Majesty'."

Now she traces the mountain chain that cups the ice sheet.

"We have sensors on the glaciers that feed the Ice Shelf, to track their movement."

She clears her throat and continues more cautiously.

"Based on the readings, I believe that a series of unusual glacial events are about to happen. The four largest, the Byrd, Nimrod, Beardmore, and Shackleton Glaciers, are about to make major advances."

"Advances?" Jay prompts.

"Yes." She appears reluctant to elaborate.

He senses they are near the end of her prepared information, so he presses. "Could you please explain, Doctor?"

Her microphone catches the squeak of an opening door and Kate Sexsmith tosses a glance off-camera. Jay clicks his teeth. Someone has entered her office. Hasn't she been told to keep gawkers out until the interview is over? At least the person has the sense to keep quiet, and his guest continues, returning to familiar, safer ground.

"Well, for example, the Beardmore Glacier is over two hundred kilometres long," Kate says. "Normal flow is about one metre a month."

"And you're expecting something out of the ordinary?" he asks.

Her attention turns to the other person in her office. She seems unwilling to go on. Jay waits. Something is up. This woman is struggling for the courage to speak. He leaves the silence open and she fills it. There's a terrible tremor to her voice.

"The Beardmore may avalanche." A cold tendril of fear touches the base of Jay's spine and she plunges on. "And the other three glaciers as well. The same. All four lie on the same geological bed, the same mountain range." She rushes on. "One event may trigger the others through a kind of resonance in the bedrock — "

"What do you mean? What kind of resonance?"

She begins a nervous explanation, but is stopped by a long, rumbling boom. The web-camera convulses, her image dances.

A bank of monitors emits a harpy's chorus of warning tones and she disappears from view, Jay and the interview abandoned.

"Doctor!" he calls.

One by one the warning tones snap off and Kate Sexsmith reappears. A printout unreels through her hands and he glimpses fresh red ink jumping across the final page. She looks into the camera.

"What's happened?" he says.

Her blue eyes are glassy, her focus inward. He knows that look. Scientists often carry virtual worlds within their own heads — models of the things they've spent years studying, waiting for, hungry for fresh data. Kate Sexsmith has withdrawn into that world; she seeks a depth of understanding only another expert might fathom.

"Doctor!" he calls again. He needs answers and doesn't want her going all "Rain Man" on him.

Into the hush the unseen gawker who entered Kate's office earlier mutters a single word. "Jesus." The voice is deep and male, and carries the accent of an Australian. The squeaky door bangs again, signaling the man's departure.

"Doctor Sexsmith," Jay persists. "You're saying — have I got this right — you're saying that if the Beardmore Glacier falls down the face of the mountain . . . "

The woman jerks back from whatever theoretical model she was immersed in and he gets what he wants.

"It falls into the Ross Ice Shelf, yes," she answers. "I'll lead a team out to the Byrd Glacier. You see, Byrd is twenty-four kilometres wide and closest — "

On the screen a broad-shouldered man, made larger by an orange parka, charges into view. He sports a beard, thick and Viking-red, and strides like a rugby half-back — strong enough to make the tackle, lithe and fast enough to carry the ball. He thrusts an identical parka at Kate Sexsmith.

"Come on, Katie." The voice identifies him as the man who was in the room moments ago — a voice that now rides the sharp edge of panic. "Come on, now!"

She doesn't take the offered coat and he reaches for her arm. She pulls back.

"What's happening?" Jay's question goes unheeded. "Kate!"

Red-beard turns. His face looms into the camera and fills the screen. Then he snags Kate's elbow and hauls her out of sight.

"Doctor? Hello?" Jay's face is numb. "Is anyone there?"

No answer. Her chair spins in the now-empty office and a different kind of emptiness settles into his gut. Ten heartbeats tick by. He ignores the frantic signals from Al in the control booth. The rotating chair slows to a stop. He struggles to face the glass eye of Camera Two.

"Startling developments on the Ross Ice Shelf." He trails off, looks down. His notes hold no answers.

"Jesus." He repeats Red-beard's comment and collects himself to continue.

"I-TV — I mean, I will, I will — "

It's the start of a promise cut short. The network has gone to commercial. In the control booth a screen displays a world of empty highways and untouched beaches where a luxury SUV roams at will, while Sting sings a love song to torque and horsepower.

Scott Base

"Let go!"

Kate twists, trying to pull free. Frigid air spills down the hallway and a knee-high cold front sweeps past them. Condensation billows around her like an incoming tide.

"Goddamn it, Lawson. Let go of me!"

The source of the cold is obvious. The double set of doors at the end of the corridor, normally an air-lock against the Antarctic blast, is wide open. A cloud of ice crystals fills the exit.

The big red-bearded man in the orange parka lets go of her and they stop. Another man, whose dark face is hard with indignation, has stepped into their path.

"What the hell, Lawson?" The dark man is Graham Palmer, the marine biologist. His work has little crossover with her ice studies but Kate knows he's not one to tolerate the chaos that fills the corridor.

Eric Lawson pulls on a pair of leather mitts. "There's going to be a wave, a shockwave," he says to them both. "In the ice."

The wall near the doors is covered with parkas on hooks. Lawson grabs one and throws it at Palmer.

"I'll get a Hagg. Hurry."

Then he is gone, through the cloud of ice crystals and out the open doors. The fog eddies and refills his passage. As Kate watches Palmer pull on the heavy winter coat she pockets her glasses and steps into a pair of insulated boots.

"What's he talking about?" Palmer is a native New Zealander. His words are clipped by the cold and by confusion.

"There's been a glacial avalanche," Kate says.

"Oh . . . " Palmer's skepticism is evident. Then he moves. Not out the open doors, but back into his office. "Wait," he says. "I'll be right there."

But she doesn't wait. She can't. She crosses the foggy threshold, stepping through zero visibility, out into the perfect clarity of an Antarctic morning.

Lawson is already in the cab of a Hagg — a Hagglund snow-crawler. The base has a half-dozen of the big snow-machines. The other five stand silently nearby, workhorses ready for another day. Each has a red steel crew cabin big enough for four. Boxy and awkward, perched atop twin caterpillar tracks, they are the last word in polar transportation.

Behind Kate the base's eight buildings are all painted lime-green, a colour meant to give the eye rest from the endless white and grey. It's been her home for eighteen months. Established in 1957 under the leadership of New Zealand mountaineer, Sir Edmund Hillary, four years after he stood on the summit of Mount Everest, Scott Base was named to honour the ill-fated British explorer, Robert Falcon Scott.

Built on a sloped promontory that juts a shale chin out into the pack-ice just a few metres above sea level, none of the buildings are far from the shoreline. The location is convenient for marine, ice, and land-based studies, and normally Kate would've said that Sir Edmund had made a good choice. But not today.

The Hagg's hot exhaust marks the air. It's a long step up from the Massey-Ferguson farm tractors Sir Edmund used on his 1958 drive to the South Pole.

People are at the dining-hall windows, curious about the early morning activity. At one frosted window she sees Ted and Eva Bowers wave an invitation for her to join them at breakfast. They are a kindly older couple, the unofficial Mum and Dad to everyone here. At another window Bill Cherry, the camp administrator, wags a finger at them.

"Come on!" Lawson yells over the Hagg's rumbling engine.

Graham Palmer hustles up. "I'm not leaving my work." He cradles a laptop computer and a case of CD-ROMs.

Kate starts toward the dining hall, to warn the others, to organize an evacuation. Seen obliquely through the frost, they might be the ghosts of Captain Scott's lost party.

Then she feels it. Not the sonic boom she heard minutes earlier, before Lawson grabbed her. By comparison, that had been ethereal. This is elemental.

Beyond a narrow range, the ear cannot detect sound, but as any rock concert fan knows, the body itself is a resonance chamber. Kate's chest trembles, a leaf in a sudden storm. For an instant she knows the shape of her own beating heart more clearly than her tongue knows the inside of her mouth.

Who could feel that and not look for the source?

Kate and the two men turn south. South, toward a marvel that is part of the everyday existence here. The cliff, a hundred metres high, thrusts up out of the ocean. They still call it "The Barrier."

It is the seaward edge of the Ross Ice Shelf.

Not a level sheet, the Shelf is an icescape where plates the size of suburban neighbourhoods shift with the seasons, shaped by the slow processes of wind and tide.

But now she can see swift movement where there should only be frozen stillness. All across the southern horizon, the edge of the world lifts. Atlas has shifted his grip on the globe and there is a shockwave in the ice.

She cannot estimate the wave's speed, but behind it the air is filled with sparkling white; a twinkling curtain composed of a billion billion pieces of broken ice, some as small as a grain of sand, some much, much larger. Each hurled, glittering, into the sky.

To know something might happen, and then to see it happen, are two very different things. In her lectures on theory versus experience she likes to quote Mark Twain, who said it's like "the difference between lightning and a lightning bug."

The wave is not a perfect line. It is the product of four, falling, runaway glaciers, thrust like goring bulls into the Ice Shelf's back. Shifting arcs move within the shockwave and where two meet, shards of surface ice are launched ahead of the onrushing swell. Launched like harpoons, catapulted forward at the speed of sound.

A twelve-foot spear of cobalt blue impales a stretch of sand near the Hagg. Another strikes a rock and both ice and stone explode.

More shards pelt down around them, a hail of needles and knives. The camp buildings' sheet-metal roofs thunder, harmonic tenors amid the oncoming roar.

More faces join Bill Cherry and the Bowers at the dining-hall windows.

Kate waves frantically but they seem confused, seeing without understanding. In the clamour a razor gash appears on Palmer's brown cheek and red splashes across Kate's boots. Then the two of them are inside the Hagg's cab with Lawson.

Kate shouts, "Go! Go!"

Ice fragments punch the crawler's roof. Lawson mashes the accelerator, the engine roars, and the boxy little beast leaps forward. First place means life but the finish line is unknown. There's no finesse to it. No question of tight corners or delicate handling. It's just scream and drive.

It's not here yet but there's no doubt — the shockwave is coming, and fast. Like a tsunami, where it has plenty of depth the wave keeps low and quick. Touching the foreshore, the front of the wave slows and the rest catches up. Catches up, and starts to pile up onto itself. In seconds it transforms great speed into massive height.

Kate shuts her eyes a moment. She and the two men are a Frost Giant's toys, given faint hope of seconds more to live. When she looks again, the wave is kneeling before the coast. It stands and stands again, teetering with power.

Then it falls on Scott Base.

Compression waves jitter through his blubber.

All sense of balance is lost.

Ring's pod rolls and pounds the waves, thrashing against the cacophony.

Frantic ripples spit droplets of seawater skyward to fall on his broad back, a salted rain. New and violent vibrations shake his body.

He has heard ice move and break before — the tickle of floes, the boom of bergs calving — but nothing like these bellowing mountains of ice.

He cannot sing against it. All pitches are filled — there's no space for tone. The uproar silences his pod. No one gives voice.

Even during the Great Slaughter this was never allowed to happen. The Blue Whale song of the ocean world has never been suppressed. Now they are overwhelmed and silent.

Even when the worst is over — for it never seems to truly end, as the reverberations echo off distant coastlines — it seems that to sing again would take a store of courage that the Blues have lost.

His father, old Milk-Eye, is the first to squeak. Not song, but simple panic.

Flee!

The call freezes Ring even as it is taken up by others of his family.

Flee!

Flee!

They turn north, whimpering, their fear as foul as a bloated seal carcass.

This is everything he hates. This is un-thinking.

Listen! he demands.

Flee! They refuse him, racing away.

It's cruel, and stupid, and he will not have it. He will not accept this loss. He must show them that fear can be faced. All along his great body he feels the ocean's direction lines change as he turns south — away from his fleeing family — to see this place where so much ice has been broken, to prove he need not always be afraid.

❨❨❨

It's hard to swallow food today. His family calls to him as they flee north. They are simple, plaintive cries, not worthy of their beautiful voices.

Come, Ring!

It's Milk-Eye, his father. There's confusion in the old whale's voice. He has lived through the Great Slaughter and suffered many losses.

Ring doesn't reply. He isn't sure he can explain what he's doing without making his father feel more pain.

To swim alone is dangerous, his father calls. To swim *south* alone is madness! Packs of black-and-white Killers roam the deep-south seas.

Ring knows a Blue pod can drive a Killer pack away by huddling in a circle, threatening the hunters with their powerful tails that can stun or kill. But Killers won't shrink from attacking a Blue on his own. They are sleek and fast. Not filter-feeders like he is, but sharp-toothed carnivores.

Despite his great size, they would take him as easy meat.

As, on a moonlit southern night, they had taken his mother.

"No way!" Jay Traljesic delivers his opinion with a well-practiced vehemence.

His producer, Al Milliken, is no slouch and gives as good as he gets, and soon their shouting match has chased most of the *Innovation-TV* staff out of the meeting room. Only two sharp-suited lawyers remain.

"This isn't about who did or didn't send Kate Sexsmith the 'no-gawkers' memo," says Al. "None of that matters."

Jay leans over the table toward the other two men. "What happened after we cut to commercial — what wasn't broadcast to the world — *that* is what matters."

"And what we're going to do about it," says Al.

Jay knows he hasn't been fair. This isn't Al's fault. The poor guy is just as angry as he is.

But this is crazy. The two tenth-floor network suits sitting in the meeting room have not stopped taking and making calls. They have names but Jay has mentally labelled them "Pinstripe" and "Solid Grey."

All the recorded footage of what happened in Kate Sexsmith's empty office after the interview is gone.

Faster than Sting's luxury SUV, Al Milliken had rushed from the control room, phone in hand, to join Jay on the set, and for two long minutes after the red-bearded man dragged Kate Sexsmith away, Jay paced and Al dialed, trying to reach anyone at Scott Base.

"Call the FBI," an assistant director suggested.

"That's just stupid," Jay snapped. "What can they do? It's Antarctica."

All the while, the studio monitor continued to display the silent, static image of Kate's empty office. Silent that is, until the drumbeat began.

It stumbled at first, a strange, syncopated beat that issued from the studio speakers. Slow, then surging, an invading army, pounding to get in. The phone call forgotten, Jay and Al turned to look at the still motionless room on the screen.

Where Kate had stood to touch the map of Antarctica moments before, something hit the wall like an artillery round. It left a ragged hole through wall and map alike, framing an eerie light-show. A sheet of jewels flickered, glinting greens and blues, until a white mountain appeared and the screen went black.

Jay shouted, "Satellite pictures. Now!"

And things went to crap.

The footage wasn't slated for immediate broadcast or for distribution to the affiliates. No, it was just gone, disappeared into Pinstripe's briefcase.

The suits had been contacted by someone in government (no names please). Someone who had decided that the footage might affect National Security (and no, you can't ask why).

In the Antarctic Ocean

Ring's aunts and uncles said she'd wandered too far, but he knew it was his fault.

Newly weaned, he'd longed to roam with Milk-Eye and the other adult males. Half their length, a quarter their size, but no longer tied to the teat, he'd wanted to explore his new freedom.

And Mother had let him go.

Until that day she'd always been so near that for him, one half of the world was Ocean, and the other half was Mother.

His father, younger then, had been the first to sense the danger and call for a circle.

From all directions, Blue males had converged to form a fortress of muscle and bone around him. Aunts and cousins had joined them and the Killers kept well back.

In a short time the hunters will move on, his father had assured him. Well-fed Blues can outlast any siege an impatient pack might lay.

But one whale was missing from the circle.

Your mother is canny, his uncles said.

She'll stay well away, silent.

With a little luck the hunters will never know she's out there.

The circling Killers soon tired of their meatless enterprise and turned away to seek easier prey. They could've gone in any direction. But chance pointed them straight at her. Milk-Eye would've gone to defend her, if he hadn't had a calf to protect.

The memory leaves Ring adrift for a long moment. Mother had been left to fend for herself. What might he do if the Killers came for him? He doesn't know. But he won't turn back.

Innovation-TV — New York

Normally, as star and producer, Jay and Al select the show's guests together. It's a point of pride to bring the scientific establishment's brightest to public attention; and a bit of notoriety can help any scientist with the next grant application.

But Jay and Al have not selected today's guest. The network has made a decision.

"He'll be a White House hack. A mouthpiece." Jay twists the cap of a magic marker, thinking of voodoo dolls.

"I can't do anything about that," Al replies. "It's a package deal. Him and the satellite photos, or no photos."

"Why can't you get pictures directly from NASA?"

"My contact said all Antarctic data has to be fact-checked by the White House prior to release."

"What the hell does that even mean?"

"He chose not to elaborate," Al says. "You know, Jay, NASA has been touchy ever since you grilled the Director about why they dropped the phrase 'to protect our home planet' from their mission statement."

"Al, how can it *not* be part of NASA's mission to 'protect our home planet'?"

"We broke records," Al says drily. "That interview featured the longest stretch of dead silence shown on network television in ten years."

"Okay, okay." Jay waves that aside.

"There's no joy from the private companies either," Al says. "Very few use polar orbits, and, for the few that do, someone has bought exclusive rights to all satellite images south of Cape Horn for the next thirty days."

"Someone with a very fat wallet, who uses 'National Security' like a mantra," Jay says.

"So, if we're going to get anything worth seeing, you've got to interview their guy." Al holds out a resume.

"Rookland?" The head comes off Jay's magic marker with a satisfactory pop. "He doesn't know jack."

"And it's got to go live." Al stands. "They want him to interpret the photos on-air, with no preview or edit."

"So whatever this jerk says, it'll look like he's got our stamp of approval?" Jay scans Rookland's resume, looking for a way out.

"You want to follow this story?" Al gathers his papers. "It's this or nothing."

"Yeah, crap." Jay heads for the door.

Two minutes later Al is in the control room and Jay is talking to Camera One.

"We're following our top story. Before her apparent abduction, live on this program, Antarctic scientist Kate Sexsmith reported that the enormous Ross Sea glaciers were on the move. Since then, our efforts to contact Doctor Sexsmith, or anyone else at Scott Base, have failed. A spokesperson from the White House Science Advisor's office, Mr. David Rookland, is live with us via satellite from Washington to give his views on yesterday's events."

"Hello, Mr. Traljesic. Oops! Sorry."

Jay turns to the monitor, where an earnest-faced man fiddles with his lapel mike.

"That's all right, Mr. Rookland. We can hear you fine. I understand you have some satellite photos to show us." Jay keeps his tone neutral.

Rookland taps a keyboard and a pair of images appears on a screen behind him. Each bears the familiar bitten-cookie shape of Antarctica and the Ross Sea. One is marked *April, 1965*. The other, the reason they've let the man on the show, is date and time stamped from a few minutes after Jay's interrupted interview with Kate Sexsmith.

Rookland reads from his notes.

"As anyone can plainly see from this comparison, in 1965 the glaciers in question extended ten to twenty miles out into the Ross Ice Shelf. That photo is from one of our earliest satellites, from back in the Space Race days. We've enhanced the contrast so that it's easier for you and your viewers to understand."

Rookland flips a page.

"Next to the old photo is an image from early yesterday morning, local time — right after you spoke to Doctor Sexsmith. I should point out that for many years, fringe scientists and the liberal media have cried wolf about global warming." Rookland's hands are frantic birds delivering derisive quotation marks.

"In fact," Rookland drops his hands, "these theorists claim that around the world, glaciers have been receding. Thankfully, as you can see in the second photo, dear old Mother Nature has proven them wrong again."

"I'm not sure I — " Jay tries to interject.

"As the photo shows, all of the glaciers along the Ross Ice Shelf have self-corrected. In fact they've even moved farther out into the Ross Sea than they were in 1965. So no one has anything to worry about."

Dumbfounded by this display of convoluted logic, Jay sees Al at the control room window holding a small whiteboard emblazoned with the words "Newton's First Law?"

It's not a warm smile that Jay offers the camera today.

"Mr. Rookland, what about Newton's First Law?"

A cloud darkens the guest's face.

"Personally, I don't subscribe to that theory," Rookland says. "I'm inclined to allow for the possibility of Intelligent Design."

"Intelligent Design . . . ?" It takes a moment for Jay to catch his drift. "No, no, not Darwin. Newton. You know, Sir Isaac Newton."

"I'm not sure what you're getting at," Rookland replies and his notebook doesn't seem to hold an answer to this question.

"Newton's First Law of Motion," Jay explains. "You know, an object in motion will remain in motion until affected by an outside force? The Ross Ice Shelf has been pushed by these glaciers. It's an object in motion — "

"I don't see your point." They are off-script and Rookland is getting angry.

"My point is, have these four glaciers shoved the Ross Ice Shelf out into the Pacific Ocean? Will it keep moving?"

"This administration believes in hard science, not theories." Rookland seeks refuge in his prepared materials.

"Newton's Laws of Motion are not theories!"

Head down and eyes on his notebook, Rookland bulls through his talking points.

"There's no consensus that global warming is real. America will not have carbon emission limits forced on it by foreign socialists. America will remain free."

He pauses for breath and Jay leaps into the breach.

"What about the eighty-five people at Scott Base? Have you heard from Doctor Sexsmith? Or anyone there?"

This at least appears to be a question Rookland has been prepped for. He visibly relaxes. Pages are flipped.

"We believe there's been some damage to the radio dish at Scott Base. Just to be on the safe side, a rescue team is on its way. We expect them to arrive on the scene in the next few hours."

Again Jay sees Al point at his whiteboard.

It now says "McMurdo — Two Miles?"

"Excuse me," Jay cuts in, "isn't McMurdo Air Force Base only a mile or two away from Scott Base? As I recall there are two thousand people on staff there. Why not just have someone drive over to check on the New Zealanders?"

The question fixes Rookland like a specimen pin.

"Yes, well, McMurdo is having some communication problems too." Rookland trails off. "You'll have to excuse me." He is gone. The connection cut.

For the second time in two days a guest has disappeared.

Ross Island, Antarctica

The Hagg is dead.

On the upper slope of Observation Hill its remains lie broken. Steel frame tubes jut through metal skin like compound factures.

Close at hand, blocks of ice lie strewn about like loaded dice. Some tumble back down the slope, toward the shore. As they roll, bits of lime-green metal, like twisted candy wrappers, appear and disappear — all that is left of Scott Base.

Scandinavians are wise in the ways of polar exploration. The first team to reach the South Pole was lead by that meticulous Norwegian planner, Roald Amundsen. It is the marriage of that great tradition with the finest in Scandinavian engineering that has produced this un-handsome child, the Hagglund snow-crawler.

On a continent ninety-eight percent covered by glaciers, it's a virtual certainty that your vehicle will hit, or be hit by, very large pieces of ice. So despite the howls from Accounting, the Hagg's designers surrounded her cab with an interlocking steel frame, a cage of roll-bars, meant to protect the passengers from harm.

And so the Hagg is dead, but three people are not. An astronomer, a marine biologist, and a polar climatologist.

Kate Sexsmith stands near the hill crest and looks down at Eric Lawson and Graham Palmer sitting on the uneven shale.

A tent huddles, half-erected against the lee of a boulder. Which of them salvaged the shelter from the emergency supplies, Kate can't remember. All is a blur of cold confusion.

First there was chaos and unbridled violence. Then silence. Pinned in the distorted snow-crawler, arms trapped above her head, she had nearly been smothered in her twisted parka. How many cold, sweaty hours did she spend in the tent, breath's condensation dripping accusations?

Now Kate staggers to the hill's summit and turns a slow pirouette, a figure on her grandmother's broken music box. The vista should show her salvation in the form of the American air force base, McMurdo, seated safely on a bay with lumpy hills wrapped around either side.

In her time here, she'd gotten to know a few of the Americans there.

The Yanks had jokingly called the New Zealand base personnel "Scotties" and were warmly called "Micks" in return, a goofy mismatch of national nicknames that offended no one.

Decades ago, with the moral certainty that comes to those who live far from danger, the New Zealand government had banned American warships from their harbours. But here, with that expansive generosity so common to the American nature, the Micks had often invited their Scottie neighbours over for drinks and Texas T-bones.

Kate had been a popular guest and more than one smitten young airman, too far from home, had proclaimed his admiration for her.

Now plates of shattered ice, the size of infields, cover McMurdo in layers of crushing death. The New Zealand base has been devastated, but here the bay has caught the onrushing wave, embracing and channelling the ice, to overlap and entomb the unsuspecting Americans. Every Mick is gone. Those poor, lonely young men. Gone.

Two thousand dead. Two thousand questions. Why didn't she see it coming? Isn't she the expert?

She turns east. Fog softens the horizon and close to the island a slurry of seawater and shattered ice churns. If only she could plunge into that chaos, scrub away her responsibility. "Out, damned spot."

Past the slurry, the Shelf lurches a hundred metres tall above the water and stretches into the hazy horizon. It slides north at speed. Shock drains Kate's face pale while she processes the implications.

In the past, pieces of the Shelf have broken off, but inertia always kept them confined to the Ross Sea. They never escaped. Now four runaway glaciers have thrust into the back of the Ross Ice Shelf. They're pushing still, and a vast fragment is surging out into the open ocean.

Lightheaded, she slumps to the ground. Shale presses against her face. That is only just. What punishment could ever balance her failure to warn them?

A lifetime before . . . before the shockwave, she had described the Shelf to that TV reporter. Now one fact plays over in her mind. "The Ross Ice Shelf is the size of France."

She lies back and consciousness lets go of her.

Beneath the Ross Sea

"We're above the thermocline limit, Captain."

"Very good, Planes."

To a submariner the universe is not a place of light and vision. It's a place of sound, and of silence. To live, a submarine's crew must listen and know all that is around them. And they must be still, an unheard nothing in a world of hunters.

Captain Clinton Rymill USN SSBN lives by that credo. He's been a submariner his entire career, save for one unhappy tour as an Ensign aboard a little destroyer. He far prefers the enveloping silence of the depths to the constant churn of surface duty.

Since making Captain, he's declined all promotions and dodged all off-boat postings. Infrequent visits to the Pentagon are enough to keep the admiral off his case and a spotless record keeps him right where he wants to be.

Except just now he is definitely *not* where he wants to be.

His boat, his command, the SSBN *Lincoln* should be many fathoms below the thermocline. Not above it. Not rising to the surface. But that is where they are headed.

"Thank you, Planes. Maintain rate of ascent."

"Permission to speak, sir?"

"What is it, Planes?"

"Begging your pardon, sir, but what dough-head decided that a nuclear missile boat should screw around with rescue operations?"

"Watch the chatter, Planes," says Hank Skelton, the *Lincoln*'s executive officer. Hank sounds worried, but doesn't state the obvious.

The *Lincoln*'s rightful station is the remotest spot on earth, as deep as she can go. Other subs might be closer to their targets, but the *Lincoln* is an ace so far in the hole that their country's enemies have to think hard. Not about America's first strike capability, but about America's *last* strike capability.

No matter what the Chinese might say about an army without end, or what plague the extremists might have wet dreams about, they all know that hidden in the ocean's depths America holds the last trump.

"Planes," the captain says, "we're not where I'd like us to be, but our orders are not open to interpretation." He looks down to find the printout crumpled in his hand. He smoothes the paper on the chart table, vexed by his momentary display of anger.

The decrypted text reads:

*Full Red Priority Order

*From: CNC SSBN Admiral G. Hart

*To: Cmdr. SSBN *Lincoln*

*Action: Conduct Rescue Operations with all resources at best possible speed

*Location: McMurdo Air Force Base, Ross Island, Antarctica

He signs it to confirm receipt and hands the page to a midshipman. Filed in the *Lincoln's* records the wrinkled paper will forever stand out from the unblemished sheets that have preceded it. That irks him all the more.

The XO speaks again. "Captain, Sonar reports no hostiles detected above or below the 'cline."

"Mafri's confident? With all the noise, isn't sonar too badly degraded?"

"Yes, sir. But Sonar Chief Mafri says it's a blade that cuts in our favour. For hunters, the grind will make a hash of things."

"Very well," Rymill says. "Let's get this thing done and get back to depth."

The ship breaks surface in open water west of the island, several miles away from the moving ice mass.

"Negative radio contact with McMurdo, sir," Skelton reports.

"Not a good sign, Hank."

"No, sir. As ordered, our radar is inactive. But there's too much fog to see anything from the sail. We could send men out in the Zodiacs, but I recommend we launch a Prowler."

"Fair enough. Orders say to conduct rescue operations, but there's no need to put boots onto the island until we know the situation."

"Yes, sir. And if the Prowler finds anything that might endanger the boat we can get the hell-outta-Dodge fast."

It makes sense to send an unmanned airplane. They might lose it but no Washington bean-counter will argue with the logic of expending a drone to keep a billion-dollar missile boat and her crew safe. In a few moments a small JATO rocket kicks the Prowler out a deck hatch and into the Antarctic haze.

The pilot is Andy Trip, the remote-control-joystick-jockey whose workstation is down the passageway from the boat's main Control Centre. He relays camera views to the CC from both the visible light and the infrared cameras. Picking out the heat signatures of buildings, vehicles, and humans against the frozen terrain should be simple, but an ice-crystal mist over McMurdo blurs everything.

Hank Skelton orders the drone lower.

The infrared screen remains grey, but the visible image resolves.

They see light prismed by ancient ice, forging gems that no woman will ever wear. Misplaced Amazon emerald greens ripple through the blocks that entomb McMurdo. At moments it looks as though the Base's lights might still shine below. But that is only a cruel illusion.

Rymill and the XO share a look, as if each man needs to confirm that another person still lives on the face of the planet.

This place is as raw as a freshly dug grave. Nothing remains to show that for five decades men have worked to turn this inhospitable scrap of land into a human settlement. Ozymandias indeed.

"XO, prepare for immediate dive."

"Aye, sir.

"Prowler pilot, make a second pass," Rymill commands. "Attempt a handoff to satellite control. If the uplink doesn't engage before we lose contact, write the bird off."

Ross Island, Antarctica

If Kate Sexsmith hadn't fallen to the ground, Graham Palmer might never have gotten up. What's the point when the world is so fragile?

Kate and Lawson, facing forward, had been looking for a route to outrun *it*. But Graham had looked back, like Lot's wife. Now he wishes that he too had been turned into a pillar of salt.

He had worked his whole life to get to this place. When he was a small boy, his father had taken him whale-watching on the Bay of Plenty, near their home in Auckland. It was just the two of them in Father's best boat. Their skiff had floated for hours among a family of finback whales and his world had changed.

Second only to the mighty blue whales in size, the fins were living islands. Not once did they frighten him. And each in turn, as though following some whalish protocol, had come close, rolled on its side and focused one huge, black eye on him. Only on him.

With each, Graham felt a question had been asked.

Do you wish to know me?

The fins had departed, unanswered, and on the way home Graham shared this confidence with his father, a man doubly challenged — a Maori in a land of whites, and deaf from birth. Without formal schooling his father had learned to lip-read in both English and *te reo*, the Maori language, and had taught himself New Zealand Sign Language.

In the skiff, after the whales had departed, young Graham asked the old man to show him how to make the hand signs for "Do you wish to know me?"

It has been their secret greeting for thirty years.

From that day forward, Graham was a whale-man and that was that. Nothing else especially mattered.

At university he had faced barriers as white as the Ross Ice Shelf, and being one of the few brown faces there was lonely. Between scholarships and summers as a guide for *pakeha* tourists at the Arataki Centre he'd earned enough to pay the tuition for a Bachelor's degree in Biology.

His father had sold off the boats and taken a job cleaning classrooms on campus to help. They shared a small flat, made quiet by the elder's silence and the younger's studies.

Then had come Graham's Masters degree, and finally his Doctorate, both specializing in cetacean studies.

At intervals women had entered his life. Attracted by his exotic good looks, in time each realized she could only place second, behind his whales. None stayed and he never chased after them.

Normally his studies would've been too specialized for the marine biology post at Scott Base. But the deep Southern Pacific was virtually untouched in the scientific literature of whales, so he had fought for the position.

Leaving Father behind in Auckland had been hard. The old man considered going back to his boats, but "That ship has sailed," he said; the summation of a life given over to his son's dream. So Father stayed on at the university as a janitor, to clean lecture halls for each year's crop of new students, to help them too, in his way.

The sacrifices had been worth it. Graham was getting real results, important stuff. His papers were read and respected around the world. So many keynote-speaker invitations came that he had a form letter ready to decline the requests. He sent the invitations to his father, to share his success with the old man.

So here Graham had been. Here, when the shockwave came. Here to see the lives of his closest friends end, while he clutched his precious data discs, knowing that he could've grabbed some of his friends instead, and forced them to get into the Hagglund.

Graham knows the human eye is drawn to movement. It's how we survived, roaming the ancient forests and plains. See the movement, see the danger.

And in those awful seconds, as the ice-wave rose and fell, his eyes were drawn to a thousand movements.

The first rogue floe, sprinting ahead of its neighbours, was flat as a hockey rink racing to find a home arena. It had chopped the residence building in half.

Graham hated his momentary thankfulness that no one had been in the residence. Everyone had been up, some at breakfast, others already hard at work.

What rational difference did that split-second make when what followed flattened the rest of the base and killed everyone he'd left behind?

His eyes felt strained from flicking to and fro across that field of destruction. He was unable to do a thing. Ted and Eva — Bill — everyone, gone. It was too much.

So when Kate fell to the ground, Graham was grateful. It was a reason to move, a reason to pretend that he could still act in this utterly untrustworthy world. He was so grateful, he felt ashamed. Still, it got him up to the hilltop in time to hear a faint whine, a machine noise in the sky.

"Hey!" he shouts at the other two, unable to articulate the simplest thought. "Hey! Hey!!!"

Kate doesn't move. The astronomer, Eric Lawson, looks up at him.

Graham points at a tiny shape cutting through the ice-fog. "A plane!"

The Lincoln

"Second pass complete." Lieutenant Andy Trip, the Prowler pilot, delivers his report. "Negative contact, sir."

The report comes over a speaker in the Command Centre. It will be permanently recorded along with the video footage.

"Make your handoff to satellite control," says Commander Skelton, confirming Rymill's earlier order.

"Aye, sir."

Rymill appreciates his XO's steady hand as an officer. Taller than most submariners, Skelton's eyes are thoughtful and intelligent; he's the kind of man the crew could trust.

The captain nods and Skelton switches his voice channel to all-stations.

"Cycle for dive," he says. "All hands. Cycle for dive."

Lights flicker red, once and then a second time, for any crewman who can't hear the command.

Rymill knows he and his first officer will share the same silent agony until the *Lincoln* is again hidden beneath the waves. But corners will not be cut on the dive. Slow and by the book will do it. His crew is experienced and no time will be wasted.

Ross Island, Antarctica

"A plane!"

As though from a great distance, Eric Lawson hears someone shouting. He looks up to see the biologist, Graham-something, pointing into the sky.

He feels hot and lightheaded. He struggles to pull his fractured self back together. His memories start to return, like snapshots in someone else's photo album.

— The equipment is second rate. At least you'll be your own boss. A man's voice.

— Awake. Alone. Waiting for the too-short spring night to come.

— You're an ill-mannered *puckeroo*. A motherly type. (Eva?)

— It's the job. I'm in a different time zone than you is all. It's the same excuse offered on several occasions. Sometimes by him, sometimes by a woman.

— This morning, headed for some sack time, deciding to make the effort to be social, he stops to say good morning to that Canadian girl, Kate Sexsmith.

Then — something bad. He sees wreckage. They've had an accident. Something he doesn't want to remember. Rather than try, he lets Graham's shouting refocus his attention. It's important to signal that plane. For now, that's enough. He can act and leave remembering for later.

He heaves himself up, heads for the wreck. Kate lies nearby, collapsed on the bare rock. How did she get here? Is this his fault? He winces down the scree. Find a flare, he thinks. Kate needs help.

The Hagg is crumpled and torn. The tube framework has snapped and the contents of the snow-crawler are a *Where's Waldo* jumble of tools, food packets, and severe-weather gear.

On top of the pile lies Graham Palmer's laptop and a scattering of his precious CDs. Eric paws through the mess. Finding a flare will take time they don't have.

Palmer's discs catch sunlight, making it harder to see what he's doing. Stripping off a mitt, he grabs one and pushes himself back out of the Hagg, bumping into Graham, who has come up right behind him.

"What . . . ?" Graham eyes the disc. "Careful with that!"

Eric ignores him and raises the silvered disc to his eye. Cold caresses his bare hand with a promise of frostbite. The wind-chill is brutal, turning minus-ten into minus-thirty. With the shock of the accident, they won't last long here.

Sighting through the centre of the disc he finds the hazed sun, bright without warmth, and flashes a circle of sunlight at the little plane.

"One, two, three, pause. One, two, three, pause. One, two . . . " he counts aloud.

No real way to make them long and short. It's as close to an S-O-S as he can manage.

The Lincoln (Remote-Control Flight Station)

Lieutenant Andy Trip shoves the control column hard right, putting his aircraft through a steep bank. But no G-forces turn his face into Silly Putty. No blackout rings fill his vision and threaten unconsciousness.

Being the remote-control pilot on a submarine is *the* screwiest flight assignment you can pull in the Navy.

Tell a fighter-jock about the intricacies of flying from inside a sub and they'll laugh in your face. Sure, the brass-hats claim that telepresence is the future of combat flight, keeping valuable pilots out of harm's way. But Andy has enough barroom scars to prove that there are dangers to being a desk-pilot that will never earn you a Purple Heart.

As ordered, he has made sure the handover to satellite control is good, but he also quietly asked the stateside operator to let him keep flying until the *Lincoln* submerges, just for the practice.

Truth is he needs it. Simulations help, but there's nothing like real-world conditions. They make you pay attention. Crash a simulator, big deal. Crash a real aircraft, BIG deal, and it's that sharpened attention that is caught now.

"Mr. Skelton, sir! Visual contact. People, sir! People!" Take *that*, fighter-jocks.

The Lincoln *(Command Centre)*

Lieutenant Trip is right. Three survivors huddle together on the hillside. Three out of two thousand. They've risked his boat and crew for three people.

"Hold the dive cycle, Mr. Skelton," Captain Rymill says. "Launch two Zodiac rescue teams. Then proceed with the dive."

"Sir?" Skelton asks.

"Getting those people offshore where we can pick them up is going to take hours. We'll resurface once they've been secured. There's nothing in my orders that says we have to stay up here with our legs spread."

"Aye, sir. Lieutenant Trip, put the Prowler in orbit over their position and confirm handoff to stateside."

"Aye, aye, sir."

The Facts

In 1976 the largest ship in history was launched. She was the *Jahre Viking*, a Japanese-built supertanker. As big as fourteen *Titanics*, she was half a kilometre long, and when loaded weighed half-a-million tons.

Too much for the Panama or Suez canals, *Jahre* was even denied entry into the English Channel. British authorities said she was too big to navigate the narrow seas between Britain and France. Since then no ship has pushed the limits beyond the *Jahre*.

Of all the man-made objects that have beetled across the face of the earth, the *Jahre Viking* was the largest.

Until now. The new record holder is two hundred miles long. A hundred miles wide. Two thousand feet thick. The Fragment has the unimaginable mass of *five-hundred billion* tons.

It was part of the Antarctic Ice Sheet. Now, as much man-made as was the *Jahre*, the Fragment has left home for good. It has entered the world of its creator.

PART TWO

Ring

The schools of krill are left behind, along with the turbulent waters that feed them.

Ring has entered the true Antarctic Ocean. It's increasingly colder and fresher at the surface as he swims south.

It's here, in the deep southern ocean, that a current runs unconfined around the entire earth.

The Great Eastern, the Blues call it, its flow constricted only where the hooked tail of one southern continent reaches toward the outstretched arm of the polar landmass below, both curved eastward as though crooked by the sixty-five million years of storms that have punched through those confining seas.

The Passage is legendary as the most storm-ridden place on the planet. Each year dozens of hurricane-strength storms lash the six-hundred mile gap between Horn and Ice. Even a whale can drown in the Passage, when the chaos of wind and water froth the surface into foam, making it impossible to draw a clear breath.

But for now, at least, Ring is halfway around the continent from that wind-beaten place.

There's a special taste to the air here, a tang carried north from the twin Smoking Mountains, which send their steamy vapors into the sky forever.

It might seem odd for a landmark to figure so prominently in the minds of a sea-bound race, but the Smoking Mountains are famous among Blue Whales for the part they played in a favourite story.

In the first days of the Slaughter, there lived a young female, Long-Throat by name, whose family made a pilgrimage to these waters each year, just to smell the fumes' sulfur bite. It was their tradition, a rub-stone that made their pod special.

The old pods were like that, not afraid to be different, not afraid of new places and strange experiences.

One year, a fleet of the hard/noisy things came to hunt, and Long-Throat and her kin were scattered in all directions across the southern sea.

Lost and alone, her young voice too weak to be heard over more than a few miles, she faced almost certain death, but for one thing — the Smoking Mountains.

Across a hundred leagues of storms and hunters, she followed the faint, bitter scent of the Smoking Mountains, back to these empty waters — to find that the remnants of her family had done the same. Though diminished, they were a pod once more.

Ring loves that pod and he loves their story. He hopes that Long-Throat's line still lives on somewhere in the ocean world.

But no kin are here to greet him.

The Slaughter scarred his race and young Blues are fed fear with their mothers' milk. Fear that never heals, never sleeps. Fight it though he may, that fear lives inside him too.

But if he can face this new fear, perhaps the old fear can be allowed to sink away.

His people need a new story — like Long-Throat's — about courage.

And though he does not feel brave — though he can foresee a dozen ways he might die before he finds his family again — he swims on as though he were brave.

Jay stalks the station's inventory shelves, hunting portable camera equipment and ignoring all pleas for proper paperwork.

"Mr. Traljesic!" Kyle, the senior inventory clerk, is frantic.

Jay builds a stack of hard-pack equipment cases until it begins to teeter dangerously and the clerk scurries to stop the collapse.

Al Milliken stands in the doorway.

"Mr. Milliken, please!" Kyle clings to the hard-case tower.

"Jay, I agree." Al spreads his hands.

Jay hauls down a mono-pod and adds it to the tower. "And so?" He jams a battery pack into a carry-all.

"And so . . . I agree," Al says. "We'll get no co-operation from network. But you can't just fly down and expect to — "

"Al, those suits stole our video. Something big is going on. This could be the story of the decade. I'm going. And so are you."

"Me?" Al's jaw hinges open, then he smiles. "You're right. You're going to need me to keep you out of jail."

Al pulls Kyle to his feet, and starts issuing orders.

"Kyle, we'll need your best telephoto lens, and a night-sight attachment. Don't just stand there. Mr. Traljesic and I are going to Antarctica!"

Ring

Blues compare the creation of an iceberg to the birth of one of their own.

Calving, they call it.

But the iceberg Ring has found bears little resemblance to any calf he has seen or can imagine. For hours he has been passing along its eastern fringe. As fast as he swims south, it swims north.

The danger it represents is undeniable. At its present pace, it will soon escape out into the open ocean where it will be caught by the Great Eastern current, and any Blue in its way will, eventually, be overrun and drowned. They'll have no chance of diving under it. They would drown before crossing a fraction of this thing's underbelly.

A new Slaughter is in the offing and the only one who knows it is him.

His course is clear. Though he's never done it before, he must compose a song of warning — to tell the pods in the Fragment's path to get out of the way before it's too late.

The song must be new — different from any he's ever heard. He can only use sounds that won't be masked by the constant grinding roar of the Fragment itself. And if sung near the surface, the wall will simply block it, so he must dive deep so the warning can reach those who need to hear it. Done right, it should speed under and ahead of the Fragment.

His breath sprays fountains and he draws deep, preparing. The song will be awkward and shrill, but he thinks he can get the sense of things across.

A final breath. His twin blowholes clench, and he dives.

Blues are not a deep-diving race. Unlike their distant cousins, the sperm whales, they seldom need to leave the ocean's topmost layer. An adult sperm whale will dive a mile straight down in search of giant squid. So when Ring dives to find the bottom edge of the Fragment, he enters unfamiliar territory.

He leaves the world of normal sensation behind. Light fades to blue and then vanishes into black. Sounds become muted. It is not a welcoming place. The pressure is cruel and presses hard against his eyes and blowholes, seeking a way in. He misses the wind-driven waves.

He begins the song of warning, pitching the tones high. It burns his throat.

Slaughtering-iceberg-swims-the-eastern-current. Like-a-Blue-to-one-krill-it-will-swallow-you. Swim-north-or-south. Nothing-outpaces-it.

Over and over, he shrieks the warning.

A pod might only hear one part, but each iteration will give them more of the message.

His breath runs thin and he rises, aching for the surface. Normal sounds return. Light appears and grows strong. The waves roll over his back and he tastes sweet air and the Smoking Mountains' sulfur tang.

The song is on its way. It will outrace the Fragment and, he hopes, save some of his brethren. Now he must sleep.

His right eye closes and the left half of his brain falls into a deep dream.

He lets his left half sleep, while the right half stays awake and takes full control of his body. When the left half is rested, it will stand watch while the right half sleeps.

But even in half-sleep the future nags at him in dreams. To give warning once will not be enough. How many pods are too far away to have heard? This will be no one-time thing. He must stay with the Fragment and repeat the deep dive, repeat the song until all Blues know to stay away.

A long swim lies ahead, but a new sound penetrates his half-sleep. A high-pitched whistle that makes his tongue ache.

The song of Killer Whales on the hunt, coming his way.

"They've seen us!"

The little plane waggles its wings, circles and waggles again. They've been spotted. Eric hands the disc to Graham and sinks to the ground beside Kate.

Her eyes are closed and a cold wind threads golden hair across her face.

"It's going to be okay, Katie," Eric says. His bare hand, stiff with cold, touches her cheek and her eyelids flutter.

"We've been spotted," he tells her. "Help's coming." Self-conscious, he withdraws his touch and gloves his hand. Her eyes close again.

Eric shelters Kate from the wind and watches Graham Palmer rescue his laptop and discs from the debris with a quiet clatter.

≪≪≪

Kate is on the hot seat in Washington to testify and the committee chairman sports the most extravagant head of hair she has ever seen on a man. Snow-white and luxurious, it's surely a three-point edge in any election.

"How is it that you know so much about the weather, missy?" Senator Big-Do says.

"Senator," she replies, "the committee has my CV."

"Yes, but . . . " He spreads his hands.

"I have degrees," she explains, "in the physical sciences, engineering, chemistry, and thermodynamics. I'm a full professor at Simon Fraser University. Your government has consulted with me on icebreaker design, among other things. Shall I list my research papers?"

"No, that's fine," he drawls. "Let's get to the point, shall we? You've testified that global warming is not our biggest problem — "

"Excuse me, Senator. That's not what I said — "

"Just a minute, missy! You said, and I quote, 'It's not the average temperature increase that is our biggest problem.' Correct?"

"Yes — "

"Gentlemen," he never turns his attention from the cameras, "I think we've heard enough." His gavel strikes the podium and the general rhubarb of departure rises.

"Wait," Kate says. "This is my dream. I get to finish!"

The committee stops in mid-flight.

"I know you're just political animals. You want simple answers. So here it is, as simple as I can make it. As the planet's average temperature goes up, the increases aren't equal everywhere."

"Yes, yes. We've heard this before." Even in her dream Big-Do must interject. "'Some places will get hotter while others will remain very cold' — "

"Exactly. The temperature gradient will steepen."

"The what?"

"Weather is all about temperature gradients. Air streams and ocean currents move because there's a difference in temperature between one place and another. The size of that difference is the gradient."

"So?"

"Think about a hill."

"A hill?"

"The steeper the grade, the faster things roll. Coast down a gentle slope and everything is fine. Coast down a steep slope and . . . "

"Ah, I see your problem, missy."

"My problem?"

"You think politicians own the decisions they make." He *smiles at her confusion. How dare he smile?*

❰❰❰

Lying next to Kate and watching over her has helped Eric recover himself.

The lightheadedness fades. He remembers everything and finds that to recover your memories is to re-experience every loss of your life.

In the years since his mother's death he has allowed nothing to touch him. Now the locked box in his chest quivers on the edge of dissolution, and unshed tears burn his throat. What is happening to him? He barely knew the other people at the base. He didn't even cry at his mother's funeral.

"Eric, you can understand things if you just apply yourself," she always said.

In sixth grade, he presented a report called "The Perfect Eclipse" to his science class. Mum helped with the diagrams.

He showed the class how, although the sun is four hundred times the size of the moon, it's also four hundred times more distant. So when you look at them, the sun and the moon appear to be much the same size. And often during an eclipse, the moon exactly covers the sun, like two quarters laid one atop the other.

All the other kids wanted to know was, "Why? What does it mean?"

He had no answer to that. Neither had the teacher. So he was told to find out and report back in a week.

He would've just looked up the answer, but Mum had other ideas.

"Let's just think about it," she said. "No books, no internet search, just our brains. That's the deal."

At bedtime, instead of the quiet fun of reading together, she asked him questions, prodding him to think for himself. It was painful but she was patient. And when his first fumbling ideas were rewarded with looks of pride, he was hooked.

"The perfect eclipse doesn't *mean* anything," he explained to the class. "It just *is*. A few million years ago, the moon was farther away from the earth and a full eclipse wouldn't have been possible. A few million years from now, when the moon is closer to the earth, it'll be more like a quarter covered by a half-dollar. It's just a coincidence that we're around just now, when it matches so closely."

The other kids didn't get it. And they didn't like it. His answer contradicted their most cherished beliefs — that they were each the Centre of the Universe and that they lived in the Most Important of Times.

Even the teacher disapproved. Despite all his work, Eric got a flat *C*.

But his mum's pride was worth a hundred *A*+s, and he never looked back. A life of science was the obvious course and then astronomy, a realm open to conquest by thought. At university he learned that in grade six, with Mum's help, he'd recreated Littlewood's law. In essence, "If a miracle is something that has a one-in-a-million chance of happening, don't be surprised when it happens. In long run, it *will* happen to someone, once in a million times."

Eric believes that. Unlikely coincidences happen all the time. But when the million-to-one happens to you; when the world kills those around you and leaves you alive, what are you to make of that?

He wishes he were twelve again. Wishes he could talk to his mother one more time. Wishes he hadn't been so far away when she had gotten sick.

"Mum, I feel so bad. Is it really only random chance that's left me alive?" The words spill out. Whispers only he can hear. It's doubt. In himself. In what his mum has given him. The grief comes in waves, like a fever. To lose the treasure she'd given him is to lose her a second time.

The Lincoln

"The catch of the day."

It's a man's voice, sharp with displeasure.

Kate Sexsmith is under a pile of deliciously warm blankets. She never wants to come out.

"Physically fine, Captain," a gentler voice reports. "Exhausted, cold. Luckily, no frostbite. The SEAL team did a great job. Our guests should be up and around in no time."

"Thank you — " Kate pulls the covers back from her face.

"You and your friends are on board a US naval vessel," says the first voice. "The three of you are civilians and foreign nationals. All mission-sensitive areas are off limits. That means ninety percent of the boat. While in the remaining ten percent you'll be accompanied by a crew member at all times."

"Mr. — "

"Captain Rymill."

For a moment, he reminds her of Christopher Plummer in *The Sound of Music.* He has the look of a welterweight boxer and that strange military expression she remembers her father using, "a forward leaning posture" might well have been invented to describe this man's stance. Though his face is lined by worry, for a man of the sea he is remarkably unweathered and that, of course, is because he's a submariner.

"When convenient to operations," the man says, "we will put you ashore. Until then, keep out of the way." He turns to leave.

Kate sits up. "Excuse me, Captain. I need to contact the families of — " She stops. "To let them know what's happened."

"Miss . . . ?"

"Sexsmith. *Doctor* Sexsmith, Captain."

"Doctor. My executive officer, Mr. Skelton, will make a report, to be transmitted in due course. What the admiral does with that information is up to the admiral. You have no out-bound communication privileges. Understood?"

In the next bed a mound of covers growls and Eric Lawson appears, beard first, ready for a fight. "Just a minute, *figjam!*" the astronomer says.

The captain looks ready to have the Australian arrested but a crewman ducks into the room.

"Mr. Skelton's regards, Captain. We're below the thermocline and the signal you requested is ready for your okay."

"Thank you, Bates. And Bates, ask the master-at-arms to see me on the bridge."

The captain throws Kate a departing glance and swings out through the bulkhead door.

White Star Tower — New York

White Star Liners have carried passengers for one hundred and forty years. And at the age of twenty-nine, Forest Langford is the youngest VP of Marketing in the oldest cruise ship company in the world.

"Our destination is a happier you." This is what Forest tells travel magazines.

"Chairman of the board by thirty-two, baby," is what Forest tells himself.

The secret to his success is the US Navy. He keeps the figures obscure, but half of his marketing budget is spent on complementary cruises for naval officers and their wives — or their girlfriends — occasionally both. Forest doesn't much care. What he cares about is inside info.

As a result, so far he's been able to re-route three White Star ships close to major naval exercises. And each time he's put a CNN reporter on the scene. The payoff is news-video, showing the White Star logo in a report from "the front lines." It's the quintessential puff-piece.

"American tourists applaud our men in uniform. News at Eleven."

With the bottomless pit of twenty-four-hour news to fill, each of those clips ran hourly for days on the network. It's been worth millions in free advertising and the Board loves the results.

Forest is certain that today's going to be another red-letter day. He has news from one of his naval buddies. Big news! The question is: does he have a ship to play into it?

"Marsha!" he roars from his office. "I want the location of every one of our ships in the southern hemisphere. And I want 'em right fuckin' now."

He rubs his big meaty hands together.

"We're gonna make history, baby!"

When Clint Rymill returns from sickbay the first place he goes is Sonar. As ordered, Hank Skelton has the boat below the thermocline. Down deep, sound can really travel and Rymill wants to listen. The XO's report on the civilian scientists can wait until Chief Mafri has given *Lincoln* the all clear.

But he has to wait. Mafri and the on-duty sonar operator, Seaman Taylor, are frozen over the console, oversized earphones clammed tight, their eyes screwed shut.

Mafri's right hand is up and cupped in his well-known "request for silence" pose. The captain has a deep respect for the man's professionalism and has learned to be especially still when he sees "Mafri's hand".

Across the control room the XO is watching, and they share the slightest of smiles. Both of them enjoy Mafri's eclectic mind.

Long seconds pass.

A bead of sweat traces a path down the small of Rymill's back. If Mafri suspects an enemy hunter sub is lurking nearby, he needs to know now. All this surface action is bullshit! That's the problem. What have they been doing up top instead of keeping to the deeps? He has to know what's out there.

He plugs in a third set of earphones. The familiar whir of the sub's air and propulsion systems are cut off, replaced with a god-awful squealing and squawking.

He checks the console. His headset is on the same channel as the other two men's. This noise is what they're listening to with such focused attention? He reaches over and jogs Mafri's elbow.

"What gives, Chief?"

"Sir?" The brief look of aggravation fades and Mafri drops his earphones.

"Report, Chief," Rymill commands.

"Sir, the noise from the breakup has degraded sonar by about sixty percent, but anyone hunting us will have worse problems, so it more than evens out. No immediate threat detected." He continues, "I'd put us in the eightieth percentile. Give us another hour and I'll know if we're at ninety-nine percent."

Rymill indicates the noise coming from the headsets. "Equipment problems?"

"No, sir." Embarrassment shows in Mafri's eyes. "Whale song."

Rymill knows that more than most submariners his sonar chief feels a kinship with the larger whale species. There are so many parallels — their shape, their natural sonar, the life beneath the waves. Any submariner has to respect a creature that swims naked in water that would literally take his breath away.

"Don't let it distract you from your job, Chief."

"No, sir. We do need to record it. As far as I can tell it's a totally new call and we'll need to share it with the fleet so they can add it to the ambient sound database."

He's defensive but adds a request.

"If you don't mind, sir, I'd like to write it up for *Oceanic*. No one's recorded a truly new whale call since the 40s."

"On your own time, Chief, that would be fine. Just make sure it doesn't disclose anything operational and have it vetted through Command."

"Yes, sir."

"Mr. Skelton." Rymill turns to the XO. "Set a course to get us away from all this ice noise."

"Captain," Mafri speaks up. "I'd advise just the opposite, sir."

"Go on."

"If we stay close, this racket will mask our transients, make it harder for anyone to hear us. Once Taylor and I work out the filters, our ears will be as good as ever. We'll have a significant advantage."

Rymill nods his consent to the XO. "Hank, work out the details. Keep clear water overhead at all times. Maintain normal launch-on-warning status."

"Yes, sir."

"Good thinking, Chief."

"Thank you, sir."

"I'll be in the mess if you need me."

Mafri disappears back into his earphones. Eyes closed, his cupped hand rises to call for quiet on the bridge.

Sonar

Mafri turns his head, looking for something lost. The whale song has stopped. An unfamiliar anxiety finds a place in his chest. He has read everything he can find on whales and whale song.

Aristotle's claim that whales could speak was passed off as legend for twenty-three hundred years until the Canadians invented ASDIC, the earliest form of sonar.

Every sonar operator worth his salt learns whale song, most just to be able to filter it out. Not him. He loves the stuff. Sometimes when the bridge is quiet and he can really listen, he feels on the verge of understanding it.

He also feels bad about some of the Navy's recent interaction with whales. The National Oceanic & Atmospheric

Administration has investigated the high-powered active sonar of naval vessels in the Bahamian main channel and found it caused internal hemorrhages in the whales' ears. That ear damage compromised their hearing and navigation. And no wonder! At two-hundred thirty-five decibels, each active sonar pulse was as loud as a one-ton TNT explosion. The main channel had confined and reflected those pulses. It must have been like being caught in the middle of an artillery barrage. In this era of government and corporate cover-up, to think that the Navy would stand up and say, "Yes, this is our fault," makes him proud of the men and women he serves with.

But it's awfully quiet out there.

He wishes he could call back, to ask, "Are you okay?"

But nothing could be more impossible.

Ring

"Ee-eee-ee!"

The high-pitched hunting cry comes again and Ring edges closer to panic. The Killers have heard his warning song. Though meant to carry under and ahead of the Fragment, some of the sound must have echoed back.

He is four times the length and ten times the mass of an individual Killer, but a pack of Orcas will hound him to death. Though he can run and he can dive, they are fast and sleek. They will attack him from all directions, nip at his vitals until he bleeds to death.

With his family, he could face down this danger, each protecting the other, using their powerful tails to punish any attacker who came too close. Alone, he is beyond any hope of rescue.

Raw fear courses through his body. His earlier courage in the face of the roar and crash of the Fragment is gone. This danger is different. It's known. It's real. It has teeth. All he wants to do is flee.

Swim! Go!

Without volition his body answers. He arches and bows through the water, faster and faster. He soon splits the waves, as fast as any Blue might hope to swim. It feels right to run. Spray flies from his massive head. His heart thrums.

It's a false hope. He knows that. The Killers are faster. It's a race they will win. And so, though he can scarcely believe it himself, he turns. Turns toward the Killers, his jaw clenched tight. Swimming at speed to meet them.

Washington, DC

Wanda Hoop keeps her head down.

She likes her job in the Science Advisor's office. Decent salary. Good benefits. Interesting work. What she doesn't like is her new boss. And her new boss, David Rookland, is in a big huff. She hears his side of a telephone conversation through the glass partition.

"Yes, sir," Rookland says. "I know the president wants a report on this iceberg thing but I'm not getting any cooperation from the brush-cuts . . . Yes, sir. I'm keeping a lid on the media. Though I can't see why anyone should care. It's just an iceberg."

Wanda hears a brief silence while he actually listens to someone.

"Well, its 4:30. I was going to go home, but . . . Okay, I will. Yes, sir. Yes, sir. I will!"

He hangs up, Wanda hears the Lord's name taken in vain and her intercom blares.

"Wanda, call up my car. And call the Pentagon. Let them know I'm on my way."

A moment later Rookland skims past her desk, his Armani suit whispering *party money and appointed power.*

"Sir? You want me to call that colonel you met with before?" Wanda knows he hates questions. It's her job to read his mind.

Rookland stops dead. She can see the cords in the back of his neck tense. Not good. He doesn't turn around.

"No, Wanda. Why don't you listen? I said, 'Let Admiral Hart know I'm on my way.' The president has authorized me to kick some Navy tailfeathers."

Wanda knows it wasn't the president who called, but why fight it?

"Yes, sir."

She hits random numbers on the phone keypad, just so he can hear them and leave. She'll look the number up after he's gone.

The Rose Sayer

"'*From Marathon to Waterloo, in order categorical*' . . . " The rich baritone echoes down the passageway.

Captain J.G. Collins checks his appearance in the mirror. It's a moment of privacy the captain of a cruise ship is not often allowed.

Uniform — spotless.

Gold braid — shining.

Beard — grey and well-trimmed.

Collins of the White Star cruise ship *Rose Sayer* leaves Gilbert & Sullivan behind and makes his entrance, the very model of a modern sea captain.

To be the Master of an adventure-cruise ship requires a wide variety of skills, both technical and social. Not only must the ship safely reach its destination and return on time, but it must do so in such a way as to give the passengers the maximum number of beautiful views with the minimum amount of seasickness. The captain must play host and listen to the opinions of an endless array of jackasses. On that score, looking the part is half the battle.

At the Captain's Table tonight the self-appointed expert is a Florida businessman named Sam Garry. Sam seems to think that his experience in discount carpet sales gives him some "unique insights into the cruise line biz."

"I don't wanna brag, but I sell over ten million a year and you don't do that by sittin' on your can." Garry's leathery Miami face challenges anyone at the table to disagree with him. "Capt'n, what you need is Kangabac. Doesn't mildew like regular carpet. Perfect for this old tub."

Collins nods sagely and wrinkles his brow in a show of earnest consideration. "Really, Mr. Garry?"

No doubt the man will go home and brag how he "told the ship's captain where the bear shits in the buckwheat" or something equally colourful. Captain Collins doesn't mind, it's all part of the job. And the man does have a point. The *Rose Sayer*'s month-long Antarctic Adventure run, south from Buenos Aires to the Weddell Sea, puts the old girl through some pretty damp weather. He makes a mental note to find out what Kangabac is.

A steward steps up to the table and clears his throat. "Excuse me sir, signal from New York."

Collins takes the folded paper. The buzz of dinner conversation dies. The guests watch in undisguised curiosity. He recognizes the drama of the moment and allows himself a pursed lip.

Mr. Garry pipes up. "Well, what's going on?"

"Ah, I don't want to spoil it, Mr. Garry." Collins enjoys a broad smile and stands to go. "If you'll all excuse me, I must go up to the bridge. We're charting a new course."

The spreading murmur of voices is music to his ears. That new VP, Langford, is an upstart, but he's right about one thing: passengers crave adventure. And he's just whetted their appetite.

Tierra del Fuego, Argentina

Places where the land peters out and the sea seems on the verge of winning attract extraordinary people.

The town of Ushuaia, Tierra del Fuego, at the southern tip of Argentina is such a place. Sheltered on the north coast of the Beagle Channel, its snug harbour collects an assortment of sailors and ships like a sieve straining the southern sea. Large ships damaged by the strains of the Drake Passage, and little ships whose captain or crew have been tested and found wanting, limp into this sheltered cove. Some recover, re-fit, and go on with their journeys. Some are abandoned to rust and ruin. And some find an unexpected home.

A Scotsman, Blair Cockburn, harbours in Ushuaia, and he has a new charter for his boat. Jay and Al tell him they want to get south and west — out into the Drake Passage to have a look round.

Exhausted from long flights and badly designed airports, they allow Cockburn to lead them down Avenue Mupai to the pier and onto the *Marcy IV*, the steel sloop that, he tells them, is his home, hobby, and business. Their gear is stowed in jig time and payment changes hands, cash only of course. They make no complaints about the cramped births or lack of creature comforts. Jay is interested to find in the small book cabinet an original copy of Bridges' *Uttermost Part of the Earth*.

"I'll let you read it," Cockburn says, "if you prove out."

"The *Marcy IV*. What happened to the first three?" asks Al.

"Sank," is the full extent of Cockburn's reply. "Cast off and we'll see what the Horn allows today," he says.

As Cockburn works the *Marcy* out of the shelter of Ushuaia, the Scotsman explains their route.

"We want to get west. But Chile owns the western half of the maze that makes up Tierra del Fuego. Chile and Argentina have too many long-standing grudges to play nice, so trying to get permission to go west through Chilean waters will take too long."

"So to get west, we first make east?" Al asks.

"Aye, down the Beagle Channel. Then still further east out into the South Atlantic until we reach international waters. Only then will we turn south. Then at last west, into the Drake Passage, to round Cape Horn." As he talks about the Horn, Cockburn speaks with reverence. His mild rhotic accent turns thick and salty. "Lads, the old sailors had a saying: *Below forty south there is no Law. Below fifty south there is no God.*" He examines them closely, looking hard for cracks in their smooth faces. "Now we're going to fifty-five south, and more."

Once out of the harbour Cockburn shuts down the engine and raises enough sail to set the little vessel surging east down the Beagle Channel, over sloping seas. Low clouds settle a stinging sleet upon them. Dog-toothed mountains line the Channel.

The Scotsman puts Jay at the helm. "Hold her steady. I'll brew a tea."

Jay grips the wheel and speaks across the well to Al. "Sank, he said."

"Well, let's hope he learns from his mistakes," says Al.

Cockburn returns with three mugs, big, steel, and insulated. The tea is black and hot, sweetened with a dollop of Kahlua liqueur for body. After a short toast to Sir Francis, he gives them his best squint.

"So lads, we'll soon be out to sea. She may become unsettled. So why don't you tell me what it is that we'll be looking for?"

"Well," Al says, "it might be easiest to show you on my laptop."

The Scotsman nods. "I've a self-steering rig to hold the helm steady and we're still in the Channel, so we'll be fine to chat below-decks for a few minutes."

The cabin is dark. Al's laptop casts the only light. He shows Jay's interview with Kate Sexsmith, then the stupidity of David Rookland. Cockburn hunches in to look more closely at Kate, then to examine the satellite pictures Rookland and the Whitehouse Science Office provided.

Jay turns the lights back on and waits for his reaction.

"I'm not as impressed as you may've expected," the Scotsman says.

"Why's that?" Jay asks.

"I've spent years in these waters. Shelf collapses are old news down here. They've been going on for twenty years or more."

"Like *Larsen 'A'* in 1995," Al says.

"And then *Larsen 'B'* in 2002. They're the most famous. The Larsen Shelf," Cockburn explains, "lies east of the Antarctic Peninsula, and the collapses surprised the science boys, twice."

"As I recall the news stories," says Al, "from above, the Larsen Shelf looked perfectly normal, while under the surface it had turned to Swiss cheese."

"Aye, summer meltwater ate holes down through the ice and weakened the structure of hundreds of square miles of that shelf. And both times a huge ice island broke free and then disintegrated into thousands of normal-size icebergs."

"He's right," Al nods. "They simply floated around and around in the backwash current of the Weddell Gyre, east of the Peninsula."

"You think we're on a wild goose chase?" Jay asks.

"Maybe." Cockburn smiles. "This will give the cruise ship passengers something to look at. 'B' brought me some business, but the bergs never left the confines of the Weddell Sea."

"But this is different," Jay insists. "The Larsens were fragile. The Ross Fragment is solid. And it's bigger too. Maybe twenty times bigger — " He catches a well-known signal from Al and shifts from advocate into his more familiar interviewer role. "Well, Captain, you know the currents here better than we do. You tell us where it'll go."

Cockburn empties his mug and spreads his largest scale chart across the table. As with Kate Sexsmith's map, it shows a top-down view of the South Pole. Antarctica is at the centre, surrounded by a school of curved arrows that chart the seasonal current variations. Cockburn's thick fingers trace the Ross Ice Shelf.

"So, a big fragment comes off — " He glances up at Jay " — or gets pushed out by the glaciers, as you say." He reaches into his pocket and pulls out a thick Argentine coin, drops it in place on the map. "Let's say you're right and it sticks together."

Jay jumps in. "The Ross Ice Shelf is close to five hundred miles further south than Larsen was. If it hasn't broken up it will be seven hundred metres thick, and solid."

Cockburn shakes his head, but his pursed lips say he might just believe it.

"Now she slides out into the Circumpolar Current." His hand sweeps the coin along in a north-eastern curve. "That's bad." He stops and steps back.

Al looks over his mug at the sailor.

Jay waits.

He and Al each have their own ideas but Cockburn has real world experience to apply to the problem.

The Scot steps forward and his chin juts. "Hard to judge, of course, thing that size. She could catch the Peruvian and grind up the west coast of South America. Or, she could shoot the Drake, swing north past the Falklands, and connect with the Benguela. That'd take her up the west coast of Africa. Then it's an easy handoff to the Gulf Stream. Jesus Murphy! Not the Caribbean!"

He picks up the coin and flips it into the air. It spins gold and silver.

"If anyone's to pay attention you'll want to get in close for your TV pictures, then."

Bull

Eight females flank Bull, four to his left and four to his right.

They are nine.

Nine Killers.

Spread out, they cover a wide skirmish line.

Something bad happened yesterday and their normal prey have vanished. All day they've hunted and found neither penguins (oily and good!), nor seals (fat and sweet!).

They heard the awful crash of ice and the ocean has been swept clean.

His pack is hungry.

HE is hungry!

But a Blue has trumpeted his presence. The call is long, and made strange by notes he has never heard before.

Bull has seldom tasted Blue, but he knows the prey. It will be a chase, and his pack will only get one feast before the carcass slips into the depths.

Each Killer might eat a third of its own weight in Blue flesh, but most of the good meat will sink away.

They thrash the water with their hunting calls to panic the prey.

Let the Blue run early. The chase will be over all the sooner.

Ring

Ring senses each individual now.

Nine hunting calls. Nine sleek shapes in the water coming toward him. The largest holds the centre. Almost certainly the male surrounded by his harem. He and they are closing at tremendous speed.

He only has one chance. One high-speed pass before the Killers can turn and match his course. Once that happens the outcome will be no different than if he simply runs and is caught. He has only one chance. Already the outermost Killers have turned to converge on him.

He growls as never before. His voice booms and krill a body length away die, broken by his vocal power.

He focuses his sonar to daunt the biggest Killer, make it hesitate for a crucial moment. Of all of them, that's the one he might have some hope of hitting. The bull might be fractionally less agile, less able to dodge his battering-ram. The bull falters. Ring's bass thrum swings across its muzzle and it shakes.

Ring throws himself forward, his tail pumps furiously. His fore-fins, held rigid, slice the water, ready to match his adversary's every move. Who is the hunted now?

The bull comes on, its sonar quavering.

The bull feigns left and dodges hard right.

Ring tries to match the move, his fore-fins pivoting to turn the mass of his body, straining for purchase. He curves his tail, his whole body, to match the Killer's turn. But he is going to miss.

The Killer is a fluke away and Ring is going to miss him.

The bull will slip by him.

Slip by and begin the attack.

So Ring opens his mouth.

The Pentagon — Washington, DC

Admiral Garrison Hart has served his country for a very long time.

Early in that service he learned how to keep contempt off his face. But the man across the desk from him is testing that ability.

"Mister Rookland," he says. "That is the second time you've threatened me with the president's displeasure." He refrains from observing that there is a big difference between the skills needed to get appointed to high office and those needed to fill said office. "The Navy is prepared to extend every courtesy to your department, but as I already told your secretary, insofar as the ice-shelf breakup is concerned, I'm waiting for a report from our assets in the area."

"By assets," Rookland gives his best I'm-in-the-know look, "I assume you mean the sub you've got looking around down there?"

"Sir, I hope you know better than to have me confirm or deny the presence of one of our ballistic missile boats at ANY location."

"Yeah, I know."

Admiral Hart is considering giving the old loose-lips-sink-ships lecture, when there's a knock on the door. A pretty young ensign snaps off a regulation salute and hands him a sealed envelope.

"The signal you requested, sir."

He ignores Rookland's audible impatience as he reads and re-reads the report prepared by the *Lincoln*'s XO.

McMurdo Base. All personnel dead. Two thousand dead. No simple ice shelf collapse. Far graver consequences may yet be in store.

His mouth feels tight and gummy.

"Mr. Rookland. Please let your boss know that I'm on my way to the Whitehouse to report directly to the president." He stands. "Margaret, call down to have my car ready." To Rookland he says, "You can tag along if you wish."

Rookland follows, like a candy-bar wrapper caught in a whirlwind.

"You've sailed then?"

Al is at the wheel while Jay keeps an eye on the rigging. Jay senses Cockburn's need to know how useful above deck they will be. Are they better kept below? A Scotsman's judgment is upon them.

"Lake Ontario," he says. "The *Thessa*, Al's thirty-foot Marconi ketch. Both of us."

Al might've added a caveat to Jay's claim but chooses instead to hold his own council. The Scotsman seems mildly pleased that they are not pure lubbers.

"Rough or fair?" he asks.

"Rough," Al answers confidently. "Thirty knot winds, three metre breaking waves."

Jay doesn't clarify that Al has spoken only for himself. The producer has never taken him out in such violent conditions.

"Ah now, me great-lake sailors, a wee test," Cockburn says, and starts to call out commands. "Man the boom vang. Test the port shrouds. Show me you know how to use the toe rail."

There's more that Jay tries to follow. Cockburn speaks rapidly in a language that sounds like English, but most of which makes no sense at all. He's able to respond to perhaps a quarter of the orders.

In contrast Al moves around the boat, confidently touching this or that piece of equipment. He makes subtle adjustments to ropes and cables that mean nothing to Jay, but which seem to satisfy Cockburn's demands for action.

"You'll do." Cockburn nods at Al, and goes below for a short time. He returns without an explanation. Then, well east of the Beagle Channel, while they are still sheltered by the tail of the Andes, he sends Jay and Al below. "Soon we'll come about for westing," he says. "Look at the book on the table. Pay careful attention to the notes and the sixty-knot line."

Below, Jay and Al find a well-worn copy of a book entitled *Van Dorn's Oceanography and Seamanship* strapped down with a bungee cord to the *Marcy*'s chart table. It is open to a graph. The margin holds what can only be a younger Blair Cockburn's handwritten notes.

Al reads aloud, "*Over a five-hundred mile stretch of water, a sixty knot wind that lasts sixteen hours will raise waves an average of . . .*" he pauses, "*twenty metres high.*"

"Holy." Jay's face loses colour.

Al continues. "*Averages are tricky things. Only the average wave will be twenty metres high. Some will be smaller. Some will also be larger. Ten percent of those waves will reach over twenty-three metres — while the largest will come within a whisker of forty metres tall.*"

This time Jay is silent.

"*These monsters are not rogue waves. There's nothing miraculous about them. In the teeth of a Drake Passage gale it's close to a mathematical certainty that you will encounter one of these twelve story mountains of water every single hour of the day.*"

Above, they hear Cockburn's shout.

"Coming about! All hands on deck!"

Ring

Closed, Ring's lips stretch back almost a quarter of the length of his body. The underside of his chin is ribbed with folds of accordion-like skin which line the lower jaw, ready to expand. They allow him to engulf a volume of water big enough to catch the krill he must eat to survive.

The deceleration is agonizing. For a Blue to open his mouth at full speed is unheard of, insane. His jaw snaps back, the hinge threatens to pop. The folds of his throat stretch and his body compresses. A slug of sea water forces its way down his gullet.

Then the Killer hits the right side of his mouth. Thrashing muscle and bone break the horned plates of his baleen.

Despite the shock and pain Ring bites down, hard.

The bull is stunned and Ring's huge, toothless mouth closes, trapping its body just ahead of the tall dorsal fin, leaving the Killer's head outside.

A shocked moment passes. The female Killers swarm about confused, uncertain about what has just transpired.

Is this some new predator? Some super-Killer? Their calls are a mix of fear and anger.

Ring knows the fear will not last for long. He raises his flukes and dives.

The Facts

Breath

Air is a thin thing compared to water. At sea-level air exerts the paltry pressure of sixteen pounds per square inch (16 psi).

Climb a six-hundred metre hill and you scarcely notice the difference. Now dive *ten* metres underwater and the pressure *doubles*.

Ten metres of water weighs as much as all the air above your head. Each additional ten adds *another* atmosphere. At a depth of six hundred metres, where blues seldom go, the extra sixty atmospheres will squeeze Ring's body with a force of nine hundred and sixty pounds per square inch (960 psi). And Ring has a lot of square inches.

Blue whales breathe differently than humans in three important ways.

The first is the lack of connection between the respiratory system and the digestive tract. A blue whale can never have something "go down the wrong way." He can swim through the ocean with his mouth wide open and not drown.

The second difference is volume.

Some people think each breath brings them a lungful of new air, but that's incorrect. At most a human expels only about twenty percent of the volume of air in their lungs.

But with each breath a blue whale exhales almost eighty percent of the air in his lungs. A human would experience that only if both lungs had collapsed.

Their so-called "water-spouts" show just how powerful a blue whale's lungs are. Outside on a cold day a human's foggy breath might reach a metre; a blue whale's spout will shoot twenty times that.

The third difference is storage.

When a man dives underwater, a third of the oxygen he uses comes from the air held in his lungs. The remaining two-thirds are stored in his blood, muscles, and other tissues.

When a blue dives, ninety percent of the oxygen he uses is stored in his blood and muscles. A mere ten percent comes from air held in his lungs.

So holding his breath is far less important to a blue than it is to a man.

Fetch

The Universe seems to love threes.

There are three things that make large waves. The first two — *velocity* and *duration* — are characteristics of the wind.

Velocity is, of course, the wind's speed. The important thing about wind speed is that the force of the wind is equal to the *square* of its velocity. That means that a twenty knot wind is *four times* stronger than a ten knot breeze.

In the Drake Passage, *sixty* knot gales with *seventy* knot gusts are common.

Duration is how long the wind blows. A short blow can't raise waves. Water is heavy and it takes time to build a ripple into a wavelet, then into a wave.

Antarctic Ocean storms have duration in spades. Driven by the eternal conflict between tropical heat and Antarctic cold, they can last for months.

The third thing that makes large waves possible is *fetch*. *Fetch* is the product of geography. *Fetch* is the distance from one land mass to the next, the distance available for the waves to build on open water.

When a tropical storm blows out of the Caribbean and slams into Florida, it has thousands of miles of *fetch* to build its waves. But once a wave strikes land, all that energy is expended. The wave goes no further. It dies. It's *fetch* that sets the Drake Passage apart from all other places on earth. In the Drake, from Cape Horn to the tip of Antarctica, no land stands in the path of the waves. East, ever east, around and around the world they go.

In the Drake, *fetch* is infinite.

PART THREE

The Marcy

"We're in luck, boys. She's north by northwest!"

Through the gale Cockburn's bellow lifts Jay's timorous heart. All three men are on deck, in black dry-suits, trapeze harnesses tight around their chests. With the *Marcy* close-hauled they climb yet another moving mountain of water.

Through snatches of wind-ripped cloud Jay sees Al grin like a Viking raider.

"Lake Ontario storms be damned. This is sailing!"

Jay recalls from the two sailing lessons he had back home that it's only waves that break that are inherently dangerous.

At the shore all waves break. They have no choice. The sea bottom rises and the waves topple forward. Anyone who's been tumbled by breakers at the beach knows the kind of force they can exert. But waves far from shore, so-called "ocean waves," no matter what their size, will not by themselves break. They are simply water moving up and down, little threat to a well-tended boat.

To transform an ocean wave into a breaking wave, a second element is needed.

And that second element is the thing that made the wave possible in the first place — the wind.

Ocean waves that grow too tall catch the wind just as a sail does, and a strong wind can topple them over onto any boat in their path.

Catch it right and tons of cascading water will come over your bows and wash the deck clean of anything and anyone not lashed down.

Catch it wrong and the boat can roll. End of story.

And here, by God, there's no shortage of wind. There will surely be breaking waves aplenty and the *Marcy*'s job must be to avoid them at all costs.

For the past hour, even in the deepest troughs, the wind has found them, and now the *Marcy* is climbing a true monster. Taller than the I-TV building in New York, it rises like something out of the Ten Commandments, ready to smite the prideful.

"Oh," Jay moans, "I wish to God that we'd sent a crew."

The sloop cuts across the monster's face, a rude water-skimmer asking for a slap.

Her mast-tip rises up into the wind's full force. Guy wires thrum and Jay sees the carbon composite mast bow from the strain. The hull cants to port.

"Step oooot!" Cockburn's bellow reaches him.

Jay looks up to see the man point at him, then point over the side.

Step out? Trapeze over the side in this?

He wants to protest but the Scotsman is no longer looking at him. No help from Al; he's been sent forward, to add weight to the bow and keep her nose from flying up when they crest.

The order has been given. Obedience is expected. Cockburn is busy and will hold the helm based on where Jay is supposed to be.

Jay stands; both hands grip the trapeze handle.

Step out.

He sits down on the lip of the cockpit, leans back, puts weight onto the trapeze wire, willing that to be enough.

It isn't.

Wind ripples his cheeks.

One knee up, and his boot heel finds the deck tread; he pushes himself backwards, away from the cockpit, closer to the gunwale and the hungry grey water.

His legs splayed for balance, body braced at a forty-five degree angle to the deck, he fights the gale, nearly all his weight carried by the harness wire and a single hound cleat on the mast. Not enough. The *Marcy* struggles. She needs him to fly.

Step oooot! Cockburn had said.

"Shit!"

Jay steps out. Both feet planted on the gunwale, outside the fuckin' boat, he lets go of the trapeze handle and leans back, perpendicular to the mast, throws both arms above his head for added leverage, straining to heel an eight-thousand-pound steel-hulled sloop, straining to overthrow a Drake Passage hurricane.

Then the *Marcy* moves. She loves it. She spills a little wind and cants back starboard, back on course, averting disaster. Grey water skims inches under his back, sometimes touching him, spray flying, but never taking him.

Jay now understands that Cockburn is a virtuoso sail-master — the *Marcy* his Stradivarius. Hour after hour, the Scotsman reads the spindrift — "spoondrift," he calls it — like a fortune teller. He cuts port and starboard by fractions of a degree, avoiding the deadly breaking peaks.

Jay is his partner in all of it. He feels the sloop's pulse through his feet. His thighs tremble with fatigue. He rides the gunwale forward and aft, eyes on the sails, on the waves, on the Scotsman, looking for signs and portents.

Once, a pink dolphin races him across patterns of foam that marble the ocean with the veins of a living giant. Whether it's real or a hallucination, he cannot say.

Whatever the old windjammers' speed record was, he is sure they've left it far behind.

Then with the passing miles the seas begin to change.

The wind still comes on as strong as before, but the wave height drops. Then drops again. From sixty foot average, to thirty and then fifteen. The breaking crests all but disappear and Cockburn calls them back to the cockpit.

Jay and Al turn to him for answers.

"Fetch!" he calls over the wind. "Your iceberg. She's real. And she's so big, she's cut the fetch!"

"The Fragment is out?" Jay can scarcely believe it.

"Aye, free of the Ross Sea, out into the Ocean."

"It's stopping the waves?" Al's grin is huge.

"Aye. Stopping the waves dead as land. We're east of it, so the wind has only the distance from your fragment to where we are to build the waves."

"How close?" Jay asks.

"Not far," says Cockburn. "And drawing closer."

"We've got to — " Jay begins.

"I know," Cockburn shouts. "Prepare to change course to two-hundred twenty-five degrees true. That's south by southwest to you Lake Ontario sailors!"

The course correction complete, Cockburn waves to them and points at his GPS.

"Lads. Welcome to *sixty* south!"

Ring

He has to kill it.

Ring has no choice. He can't let the bull escape.

He has to go deep and stay down until this Fury runs out of breath.

He has to drown a whale.

The Killer's head protrudes at an awkward angle from the corner of his mouth, placing them almost eye to eye.

Diving, Ring sees the manic look in the bull's black orb for a few moments, then the sunlight dies.

He understands perfectly.

I live, you die.

Ring's mighty flukes force them deeper.

All light disappears and he is blind again.

But with the Killer in his mouth he cannot form the sounds he needs to see. This is complete and utter blindness, a building horror.

Anything might swim out of the darkness.

Bull

Into that darkness Bull screams his rage and a thin stream of bubbles escapes, dribbling from his blowhole.

An unfamiliar shock silences him, a thin jet of seawater sprays down his airway. He clenches hard to stop it but the Blue's insane grip distorts his spiracle and the pressure is climbing.

He has to stop it. It's escape now or die.

He arches violently, pumping up and down, makes slight gains, but loses more air, takes on more water.

He feels the Blue weaken. He should have slipped free. But his tall, proud dorsal is caught and holds him back a few precious moments longer. Twisting hard, he is out!

Mad with frustration, Bull turns to sink his teeth into the prey's long, delicate fore-fin. His jaw aches for the taste of blood and retribution. His teeth close, but only on water.

He lunges again. Ready to cleave the Blue's passing tail. Still his aim is off — too low.

How can that be? He's never missed prey before.

Then he senses it. It's the weight. Though his lungs still hold air, too much water has forced its way in. He has lost precious buoyancy.

Now the Blue is above him, rising away.

Desperate, Bull strikes for the surface but his nose will not come up. His whipping tail drives him faster forward, but he drops farther and farther, arcing down. The abyss beckons.

Now the Blue is forever beyond his reach.

With so little breath Bull has no death-cry.

He knows what's to come. He'll die and his body will become whale fall. On the deep ocean floor, in the slow, cold waters, his carcass will feed tubeworms and the like, a temporary stepping stone between the hydrothermal vents where such creatures live in endless darkness.

Silent and blind, Bull falls into the void.

Ring

Broken pieces of baleen drift past Ring's flanks, tribute to his vanquished foe. He cannot stay down any longer. He needs air.

The eight females remain above, gnashing the sea in anticipation. Their confusion has waned, they circle confidently, as cocky as the bull. Ring knows that he cannot repeat what he has just done. He knows that they will kill and eat him, and not in that order.

He knows it. But perhaps they do not.

He turns surface-ward and rises from the depths in a final burst of speed, trumpeting.

I have slain your male!

They won't understand, but the tone and volume of his bellows convey the threat.

I've eaten your bull! You're next! Swim! Flee!

Against all expectations it works. The females flee north.

Ring hears their bickering chirps and imagines them reassuring one another that they aren't afraid. That this Blue is just too much trouble. Besides, they have to find a new male, don't they? Bull was all right, but they can do better.

Ring lies silent at the surface and listens to their squabbling fade into the distance.

Milk-Eye will never believe this.

Ring will never forget the sickness of being a killer. Spent, he sleeps again, two long half-sleeps, and drifts east in the Fragment's wake.

The Marcy

"Luxury."

That's Cockburn's assessment. Al had gone below to rustle up some grub and returned with hot tinned stew.

"For the *Marcy*," Cockburn admits, "in these seas, a hot meal is not a common event."

They finish things off with mugs of hot, sweet coffee.

"This is a life worth living," Cockburn declares.

Though every muscle aches, Jay agrees. As the sun falls toward a short Antarctic spring night, the wind drops and

Cockburn sets the night shifts. It seems that they have earned his trust, at least on these lesser seas. And right now that means more to Jay than all the TV awards that line his shelves back home.

"Al, you take a reduced first watch, a three hour stint by yourself, while Jay and I sleep. Then Jay will do the same. I'll take over again at dawn. Nothing fancy's wanted. You understand, lads?"

"Yes, sir," they both chime.

"Keep her on a beam reach with what's aloft and you'll be fine. Wake me if you hit something."

Cockburn goes below. Jay shares a wordless nod with Al, claps him on the shoulder and leaves him at the wheel, temporary Master and Commander of the *Marcy IV*, to sail the Drake Passage alone. He is a bit jealous. But his turn will come.

White Star Tower — New York

"Mr. Langford, the Board will see you now."

The summons to the thirtieth floor was unexpected and unwelcome. Forest has important things to do. But an invitation from the Mandarins is beyond even his power to refuse.

Opulent, as only a place paid for by shareholders' money can be, the White Star boardroom is a naked display of wealth. The table, a continental shelf of Italian marble, is dominated by a fleet of butter-soft leather chairs. All are occupied, blockading that flat stone isle from interlopers.

Forest badly wants a place at that table, so he stands like it doesn't matter.

The men, and they are all men, are each attended by half a dozen toadies, like Medicis with their household guard.

"Gentlemen. How may I assist you?" Forest hopes they can cut to the chase.

Every face, save one, turns to him with a look of mild expectation. The remaining visage, a patrician, proudly alone at the head of the table, drips condescension. It's the chairman, Robert Bell, Junior.

"Ah, Forest, I was just explaining to everyone how well things are going on your little iceberg project."

Forest shows his teeth — a facsimile of a smile. "Hello, sir. Good to see you."

He assumes that Bell must have an informant. The prime suspect would be Marsha, his own assistant. He makes a mental note to do some housecleaning.

For six generations Bell's family has chaired White Star. His father, Robert Senior, finally died and now at age fifty-eight it's Junior's turn. With his mummy gone and no siblings he has inherited the entire family fortune.

Forest knows that he is the one shadow to Junior's otherwise happy ending; along with everything else, Junior has inherited his father's last hire, the crass and far too young VP of Marketing, Forest Langford.

Bell Junior's opinion of him is no secret. "White Star is crystal and linen. Langford is plastic and paper," to quote the great man.

Meetings between the two of them are often scheduled, to be invariably cancelled by Bell at the last moment, a trivial game meant to annoy. After nearly eighteen months in the big chair Robert Junior has granted him exactly zero face-time. Fortunately, success has bought him enough popularity with the Mandarins to prevent Bell from simply firing him.

But something is definitely up. He smells blood in the water. Robert Jr. has decided to strike, to play some angle on this iceberg thing. So he keeps silent. Best to let the chairman spring the trap. Later he can redirect events to his advantage. To struggle now will only make him look weak, and the Mandarins despise the weak.

"I'm all about the big picture," Bell addresses his peers. "But Forest is so good with the little details."

"Thank you, sir."

"Forest," Bell continues, "with so much at stake I've recommended, and the Board agrees, that we need our top details man on the scene, ready for action. The helicopter's on the roof. Your flight leaves JFK in fifty minutes. You catch the *Rose Sayer*. I'll fax instructions to the captain." Robert Jr. checks his manicure. "Well, off you go then. We'll see you in what? Two weeks?"

Two weeks. Two weeks away will kill his career. Bell will reassign all his projects and Dilbert's Law will apply. Others will take credit for any that succeed, while he will be blamed for any that fail. He wants Junior's throat in his hands, or better, his balls.

Instead he stands straighter. "Thank you, Robert," he says. "Gentlemen, I won't let you down."

As he leaves, one of Junior's protégés takes his place.

"Gentleman, this is William Savoie of the Vineyard Savoies. With Forest away . . . "

The door closes and the dismantling of Forest's department no doubt begins.

Five minutes later he is on the helipad, on his way to join the *Rose Sayer*, on his way to meet the juggernaut.

"Good food is essential to morale."

Eric Lawson and Graham Palmer merely nod over their plates at Doc Imola's comment but Kate appreciates the small talk.

After their ordeal, ordinary social interaction is just what they all need. The ship's mess is a busy place, full of the sounds and smells of normal life. She likes it.

"Confinement inside a steel drum," the doctor continues, "even one as comfortable as the *Lincoln*, can dull the mind. Our five senses so dominate our brains that CAT-scans can detect permanent changes in the brain structure of longtime crewmen."

"Like you?" Kate makes an attempt to contribute.

"Twenty years, next month." Imola welcomes her help. "Tastes and smells are a comfort to the soul and a stimulus to the mind. The taste centre in my brain is probably ten percent larger than yours. Not that I'm bragging."

"We're used to good, plentiful food," Kate says, "But the *Lincoln*'s mess is extraordinary."

"Have the cooks made a special effort for us?" Lawson asks.

"No, sir," Their guard, a thin young seaman named McNally, speaks up. "This is standard grub." McNally wipes up a second helping of beef stroganoff with a thickly buttered slice of bread.

Kate can't help staring at his holstered sidearm. He catches her at it and looks uncomfortable. She isn't used to guns. This one is thick and black, all business. She decides guns are even uglier when you know they're meant to keep you in line. If staring makes McNally uncomfortable — well, too bad.

Cutlery rattles and McNally's bread flies. It smears the floor, buttered side down, as the young guard leaps to his feet. He fires a sharp salute at the door.

"Captain! Sir! Prisoners all accounted for, sir."

Finished with the salute, McNally's hand finds the butt of his pistol, ready for action. His thumb spreads a brown dollop of stroganoff across the diamond crosshatching.

The friendly human noise of the mess dies.

"Jesus . . . " mutters a cook behind the counter.

Captain Rymill is inside the mess-hall doorway. The surprise on his face is replaced with a carefully constructed neutrality as he coolly examines McNally and then counts aloud. "One. Two. Three." An enumeration of Kate, Graham, and Eric. "Not 'prisoners,' McNally."

"Sir."

Doc Imola says, "I brought them up to eat, Captain."

Graham Palmer rises, coffee cup in hand. "A toast. I give you Captain Rymill, the Founder of the Feast!"

Puzzled crewmen look expectantly at their captain. Kate feels the tension dissipate. No insurrection seems imminent. Graham slurps his coffee and McNally sits down sheepishly, avoiding his crewmates' glares.

Rymill fills his plate at the chow-line. He does not join them. He takes a seat some distance away.

"It's the captain's custom to eat in the general mess," Doc Imola murmurs, "rather than to separate himself from the men."

But Kate sees the crewmen give him his privacy, a quiet shift that leaves a buffer zone around the captain; he is as taboo as any Hindu Untouchable.

She feels unanticipated sympathy for the man.

On an impulse she rises and crosses the room. She's been kitted out of the ship stores with a pair of trousers and a snug short-sleeved shirt and feels her approach to the captain's table draw a dozen admiring looks.

"I'm aware of the sacred space I'm about to violate," she says to Rymill, "but I hope that rule doesn't apply to outsiders. May I join you?"

Her request is quiet, meant to set a tone of conversation, not confrontation.

The captain assents. She smiles. He speaks first.

"Your colleague knows his Dickens." He indicates Graham.

"How so?" Kate asks.

"That's Bob Cratchit's toast from *A Christmas Carol*. His toast to Scrooge. I'm not sure if the implication is going to earn your friend very much of my good will."

The tone is tough but his wink catches her off guard.

"Aren't we prisoners, Captain?"

"Not as such, Doctor. McNally misspoke. But you don't have security clearance to be on this vessel. Even American citizens in your situation would be supervised at all times."

"By an armed guard?"

Rymill holds up his hands. "SOP. Anyone would be treated the same."

"How very democratic."

"Democracy is what we're defending, Doctor."

Kate recognizes a topic that isn't open to debate and changes the subject.

"Your ship is safe then, Captain?"

"Boat. Yes. I apologize for my abrupt manner earlier. You understand, pressure."

His expression softens to clarify that this is an old submarine joke.

"Of course . . . "

"And," he says, "Mr. Skelton's report has been sent. I expect Command will inform your families that you are safe. And notify the other next of kin . . . "

His kinder tone shifts back to neutral.

"But, because you're on the *Lincoln* your whereabouts will be kept secret. Our patrol won't be finished for several months. Barring emergencies, during that time I'm expected to keep the boat at suitable depth for operations. If I can safely offload you to another naval vessel, for an earlier return home, I will be happy to do so. Until that time you and the others will have to adapt." He tries on a smile that could use some practice. "Perhaps you can catch up on your reading."

"Captain, do you understand what's happened up there?" Kate's vision clouds at the memory of chaos and death.

His doubtful look brings back her steel.

"Google me, Captain. Check my credentials. Doctor Kate Sexsmith, Simon Fraser University, B.Sc., M.Sc., PhD. I'm an expert on the polar ice caps. I need to report on what's happened to the Ross Ice Shelf. The world needs to know. Your government needs to know. If I'm right, the consequences of this event may make Hurricane Katrina look like a sewer back up."

"Doctor Sexsmith." Rymill is cooling. "I'm sure my government will carry out a thorough investigation and take appropriate steps. Now if you'll excuse me."

He doesn't get up and Kate sees his outstretched hand directing her line of retreat. She's been dismissed. She wants to protest but Rymill has hunched in, like someone who's heard something that cuts too close to his heart. He returns to his meal and she withdraws.

David Rookland knows the White House is filled with gatekeepers, those unelected officials who control access to the powerful. By filtering the ebb and flow of information, they too gain power. It's what he's always aspired to.

And it's clear that those gatekeepers are one of the things Admiral Garrison Hart truly hates about the place. Riding along with the admiral, Rookland discovers this fact and he also learns firsthand just what happens when an irresistible force meets an immovable object.

It gets redirected.

The admiral's calls from his Pentagon car-phone are transferred again, again, and yet again within the Byzantine labyrinth of presidential special advisors.

Urgency succumbs to exasperation, and that grows to barely controlled outrage.

"Goddamn it! Do you know who I am, you plutocratic imbecile? Don't you think the president might want to get a firsthand report from the commander of his nuclear submarine force?

"No, I do not want to file it in triplicate for your review and pre-approval.

"No, I do not know how hard the president has been working lately.

"No, this is not a matter for proper channels.

"Look, you jumped-up political bagman — no, don't transfer me!"

By the time the Pentagon driver pulls their car into the west portico, Rookland estimates that Admiral Hart has made at least three lifelong enemies and cut his chance of promotion during the term of this administration to zero.

Apparently one of those jumped-up bagmen has called White House security. Four uniformed officers step forward, working hard to look like an escort. Rookland guesses that it isn't every day that they're ordered to detain, er, escort an admiral.

He waits in the car for Hart and his security entourage to depart, then follows from a safe distance. He desperately wants to be in on any meeting with the POTUS, but if this is going to be a trainwreck he doesn't want to be associated in anyone's mind with a runaway admiral.

The trip is short. The guards lead Hart just inside the building and take an immediate left through a narrow door into a secure waiting room.

Not a good sign. In fact, that's it, that's the deal-breaker. Rookland breezes past, eyes front, a man headed on an important mission.

"Mr. Rookland?"

He knows the bourbon-smooth voice. It is well known to any Washington insider. His bowels loosen and he reluctantly turns to face the bald, middle-aged pitbull of a man who has spoken his name.

The meeting room door frames Norman Butchart, the administration's political mastermind.

This man has reshaped the modern political world. At the age of five, it's said, Butchart read Machiavelli's *The Prince*, and laughed.

"It was," the little boy told his father, "a very funny story."

≪≪≪

"Mr. President."

"Norman Butchart. How's my favourite 'gator? The waters murky enough for you?"

95

"Just right, sir."

"Looking after our friends?"

"Yes, sir. I must say, our political base is a needy old bitch."

"She does love attention. What are your targets today?"

"The usual, sir."

"Issues to be re-framed and re-tried in the court of public opinion?"

"Must keep the opposition focused, sir."

"Not that I care if these issues make any headway, Norman. I see no need to "fix" our divided nation."

"Sir, I believe that where Karl Rove went wrong was not to have his equal in the Oval Office."

"Are we equals, Norman?"

"Perhaps more like complementary parts to a greater whole, Mr. President."

"Complementary. I like that. Remember, my friend, the truly admirable thing about the American public is its deep and abiding trust in democracy."

"And democracy hands power to those who know best how to engender distrust."

"All we need is to keep alive the issues that mobilize distrust. You know, your father tells a lovely story about a much younger you, Norman."

"*The Prince*, sir?"

"What? No. About 'The Boy Who Cried Wolf.' You thought the boy would've done better if he'd just varied the species. First a wolf, then a tiger, a lion, a bear and so on."

"Yes, sir. The variation would have done the trick — without losing voter confidence. Most voters use their vote to keep our country safe from the horrors of . . . 'blank' . . . and we just keep filling in the blank."

"Give people ever fresh reasons to vote *against* the other guy and you've won."

"May we turn to a new problem, Mr. President?"

"Yes, Norman."

"I received a call about Admiral Hart. He is demanding to see you about an iceberg. Naturally I offered to field that foul ball."

"Environmental problem?"

"Perhaps. It can create the wrong kind of public concern."

"Fear that's not under our control?"

"Yes, unchecked, that could hurt our people in the upcoming election."

"So?"

"So I agreed to take a meeting with Admiral Hart and a Doctor Rookland."

"Instructive?"

"I'll work out the details, but we'll have uses for them both."

"A standard scenario?"

"Yes. Force a leak, turn the story into an investigation of the leak — "

"Rather than an investigation of the event. Is the admiral passionate?"

"The admiral wanted so badly to see you himself, Mr. President, to explain the problem."

"Good. The kind you'll believe is a leaker."

"I've asked him for time to investigate and work on a plan of action."

"That would hit the right note with a Navy man."

"I'll put him off for a few days — "

"To build the pressure."

"Hart has knight-errant written all over him."

"All you need to do, Norman, is to provide the windmill. What about the other one?"

"As a science drone, Rookland will be given the job of writing a report for you, sir."

"Which will take just long enough to force the admiral to leak the story."

"Then I'll produce a report no one will read, disclose everything, and in the process change the story. If there's a hint of 'environmental disaster' we'll focus attention on the 'disloyal military man'."

"Heck, Norman, I might even get a job approval bump."

"Your hurt and innocent routine is the best, sir."

"The destruction of McMurdo Base will have to be reported immediately of course. No survivors? We're sure?"

"Yes, sir. Nothing politically dangerous there. Natural disaster strikes, concern for the families, our brave men in uniform, national day of mourning, blah, blah, blah."

"A bit of the old wrinkled brow and some earnest head shaking?"

"Exactly, sir. There are the kiwis, but we're taking care of that."

"It gives me genuine satisfaction to work with you, Norman."

"Thank you, sir. It'll all play out in a month and the public will have forgotten the issue long before your re-election."

"Ah, yes. Remember, Norman, life is good."

The Lincoln

2:00 AM.

Nightmares wait for Graham Palmer with fishhook hands. Kate and Eric are asleep and the gun-happy McNally has nodded off; Graham doesn't care to wake the boy. He gathers his things and creeps out.

He thought Rymill's thugs would confiscate his laptop, but the master-at-arms is a decent sort. At least there's one sane man in the bunch.

A short corridor brings him to the mess hall. It's alive with sailors, off watch. A cook hands him a coffee. He finds a corner and ignores the curious looks.

It's good to work. He keeps the volume low. Listening to his whale song recordings is a tonic. The blues and fins reconnect him to the real world. The waveform graphics on the computer screen are a puzzle, shaped out of sound. He gives them his complete attention.

After a while he looks up to find a sailor sitting across the table leaning over an empty plate. The name badge says *Mafri*. He captures his coffee mug and takes a pull. Stone cold.

"Sorry to disturb you," the sailor — Mafri — says. "I came in for breakfast and heard your recordings."

Graham chooses not to respond.

"Mafri. I run the sonar crew." The sailor holds out a hand.

"Palmer." Graham gives in and takes the hand. "Graham Palmer."

"Palmer? As in 'Whale Information Exchange'? That Graham Palmer?"

Graham nods.

"I don't believe it. Wait." Mafri rises. "I've got something you'll want to hear."

Graham shrugs at the lack of an explanation and the man leaves.

In a moment he is back. "Here. Take it. Listen."

Graham pops open the tray and drops in the unmarked CD.

An urgent whale song plays.

"Where'd you get this?" Graham asks.

"Come on." Mafri laughs. "I'll lend you some earphones."

The Pentagon — Washington, DC

Admiral Garrison Hart paces his office in tight steps.

He has been watching the White House press secretary tell the public about the McMurdo disaster on CNN. The man on the screen ends the speech with a well-worn admonition.

"We ask only that the media refrain from using this national tragedy to help further the far Left's political agenda. When you do that, only the eco-terrorists win."

"What a moron," Hart mutters. "What a farce."

There's been no mention of the bigger problem. He can see only one reason to hide the Fragment's existence and its implications.

"It's Butchart. Worried about the November midterms."

The pacing stops and his arms cross, pulling his shoulders into a hunch. He'll have to act through an outside channel.

"Leak" is such an ugly term, especially to a navy man, but the president's advisor has left him no alternative.

He knows a journalist he can trust not to divulge a source. The difficult part will be to not get caught. Can he release just enough information to get the story going without giving himself away as the source?

Butchart will suspect him, of course.

He looks at the wall beside his desk. A lifetime of awards and commendations surrounds photographs of the three presidents he has served. None of them were perfect, but only the current one has made him truly uneasy. He goes to the door. It's been a worthwhile career. He's served his country well. Now it's time to take a risk.

"Shirley. I'll be out."

The Lincoln

"This way."

Chief Mafri leads Graham through the warren of electronic panels that make up the *Lincoln*'s bridge.

"The CC is always fully staffed. The captain and XO are off duty, but a boomer never sleeps." He points. "That's Lieutenant Prudholm, the boat's Second Officer. He has command."

Thick books cover Prudholm's workstation.

Mafri lowers his voice. "Ship's regulations. He's studying. Failed the Ship Masters exam. Once more and he can kiss any hope of promotion goodbye. I give even money that he'll be in civvies when his current enlistment is up."

They join the on-duty sonar operator.

"This is Brandon Taylor," Mafri says. "A longtime shipmate of mine from Maine. Brandon, Graham."

Taylor raises an eyebrow which the chief answers with a finger to the lips, then takes over the backup station and hands Graham a headset. "Real time," he says.

"Okay." Graham says. Then, "Nice. The fidelity is uncanny."

"Now watch." With a magician's flair, Mafri produces a gold-coloured cable and connects Graham's laptop to the raw sonar output.

"Not worried about viruses?" Graham asks.

"One-way connection only," Mafri says. "I can feed your laptop from the sonar system but nothing can flow back up the data stream. No chance of compromising the boat."

In moments, live underwater sounds are being fed to Graham's PC and translated into two-dimensional wave patterns on the laptop's screen.

"A marriage made in tech heaven," says Mafri.

"Nice," the scientist says again.

Mafri whistles softly. "But no whale song," he says. The sonar-man switches from the live stream to the recorded blue whale song he shared with Graham in the mess hall. "That was live. This is Memorex."

Both men watch as the eerie melody traces a Northern Lights' dance across the laptop monitor. Hints of momentary meaning appear and vanish.

"Beautiful," says Graham.

Then on the submarine's main sonar display an image catches his attention and his heart skips a beat. They are three-dimensional.

"Chief, would it break any regulations if I patched your 3-D imaging code into my waveform program?"

Mafri pulls a manual from a shelf. "Let's see. That particular software component is commercially available. It's not cheap."

"Okay." Graham nods.

"Downloading it onto your PC would be considered software piracy." Mafri looks over to Taylor. "As sailors we take piracy pretty seriously, don't we, Brandon?"

Taylor snorts.

"Okay," Mafri says, "promise to pay the software license when you get home and send me a copy of the receipt. Do that, and it's all yours."

"Agreed." Graham is over his keyboard, ready to integrate the 3-D code into his system. The golden cable does the rest.

"What's the idea, Professor?" Mafri asks.

"Well, except for words like 'sizzle' that retain some connection to the sounds they represent, all human languages are abstract." Graham points at the main screen's 3-D display. "Since whales use sonar to see things, might they have a primitive language based on the images of the things themselves? You see?"

The next watch is taking its place on the bridge by the time the integrated program is ready to test. Graham opens a new window. Brandon Taylor has stayed to watch Mafri stream the new song.

The sounds come through their headsets and the same blobby shapes appear on the laptop's screen. Then Graham engages the 3-D software, slows the image fade rate, and the shapes become immediately recognizable.

A swimming whale, with surprising internal details of the slowly pumping heart and lungs.

Then a long shape with turbulence issuing from one end — no internal details — the hull of a ship? The whale again, pierced through by a harpoon — in pain, dying.

Then in quick succession: an iceberg; a blue whale near the iceberg; the whale morphing into a shrimp — all swallowed by the iceberg.

These simple images fade and the screen is filled with a pattern of lines, as detailed as any Admiralty chart, of what can only be a map of the Antarctic seabed covering hundreds of square miles. The map shows tiny whales swimming north and south out of the way of a huge oncoming iceberg.

The map fades, leaving a ring of air bubbles rising through water.

A long moment passes.

"Mafri?" The trio looks up to find Captain Rymill staring at them. "What the hell is that man doing on the bridge?"

"Want a list of my complaints, Graham?"

"Not really."

Eric stands in borrowed Navy pajamas. "I haven't had my morning coffee. The sailors who frogmarched me into this paint locker were a bit rough." He rubs his jaw and continues. "Our makeshift jail is cold. And our female cellmate seems to have a serious case of claustrophobia."

"Let — me — OOOOUT!" Kate Sexsmith's scream is emphatic.

"No dainty little thing, our Katie," Eric observes. "Your scream would scald a herd of Galilee swine, sweetheart. Good to know about a woman, before you get too enamored."

"It's not my fault," Graham says.

"That's one theory, Graham. I've heard it several times before. But I have serious doubts that there's much evidence to support it." Eric pulls three large paint cans off a shelf, for seats. "What happened?"

"The sonar chief, Mafri, invited me to the bridge."

"Oh?" Eric says. "Kate, you don't want a ten-gallon seat? Perhaps something smaller?"

"He's interested in whale calls," Graham says.

"That would explain it all, I'm sure." Eric rearranges the cans.

"And we've made a discovery."

"Isn't that great? Katie, did you hear the big news? Graham has made a discovery."

"It must be similar," Graham says, "to the way photographs or movies are processed by the human brain. They're just dots on a piece of paper or flickers of light and shadow on a screen. It's our brains that compile the information and extract meaning."

"I have no idea what you're talking about." Eric tries out his seat.

"Let — me — OOOOOOUT!"

"Good one, Katie. I think you hit an A-sharp that time."

"I need to run the other discs, start a lexicon," Graham says. "But Rymill took everything." The marine biologist explains all that he and Mafri saw on the 3-D computer screen. "What do you think?"

"Could be a warning to his mates," Eric says.

"Yes." Kate has stopped shouting and has become engaged in the puzzle. "He's saying 'Death is coming. An iceberg that makes a whale look like a flea is coming. Swim north or south to get out of the way.'"

"I hope he has more luck than I did," Eric says.

Graham and Kate are silent.

"Scott Base," whispers Eric.

Kate touches Eric's shoulder and mutters, "It's okay."

"Sorry," Eric says, "Graham, how can we help?"

Captain Rymill

Rymill sits in the privacy of Doc Imola's cramped office. "This really isn't a good time for a session. You know that, Doc?"

"It never is, but it's got to be done." Imola consults his clipboard. "One more tick-box for all the key-carrying officers, Clint."

"Okay, but let's make it quick."

"Sure. Command has sent me some new questions. And you know they won't want to see any one word answers."

"Okay, Doc. You're the Doc."

"Clint, tell me what it took to achieve your rank."

"You mean courses and training?"

"No, they're looking more for the qualities."

"Well, you have to be a person of keen intellect."

"And . . . ?"

"And imagination."

"Okay. Tell me the most important thing about your boat."

"The *Lincoln* carries sixteen MIRVs. The warheads are the equivalent of about three thousand Hiroshimas."

"Hiroshimas?"

"Yep, might as well call a spade a spade, right?"

"And can you summarize your job?"

"Well, sure. If a doctor makes an error, his patient may die."

"It happens. It's happened to me."

"Well, in a nutshell, when the day comes, if I make *no* mistakes, I'll deliberately kill millions of people in the name of my country."

"Does that sound insane to you, Captain?"

"Is that on the questionnaire?"

"It is."

"No, Doc it's not insane. It simply requires discipline."

"Describe discipline."

"Now I know that's not on the questionnaire."

"It's a follow-up question."

"Discipline means denial."

"Denial of what exactly, Clint?"

"History."

"You want to stick with a one-word answer?"

"To be an effective boomer captain you must be prepared to ignore a simple historical truth."

"Which is?"

"That today's enemy may be tomorrow's ally. Often within a single generation foes become friends. In the 1940s we fought Germany and Japan. Now they're our allies. To captain a boomer you must hold within yourself the capacity to, at any time and without hesitation, incinerate people who, within a generation, might be your friends."

"I see. Any fear you might be tried for, say, conspiracy to commit genocide?"

"No. It's possible of course. And to do this job you have to recognize that 'I was only following orders' isn't a defense. Are we done?"

"Nearly. Clint, given all of this, how does the Navy know you'll obey a launch order?"

"We're tested. Regularly. Blind tests. Each time, there's no way for the XO and I to know if entering the launch codes will merely record our willingness to follow orders, or . . . " Rymill shrugs.

"Now, how many 'launch on command' tests have you and Commander Skelton executed to date?"

"Four."

"Your opinion of your XO?"

"Hank's a top-notch officer. Best man I've ever served with. Are we done now?"

"Sure. Thanks, Clint. That'll cover things for now."

The Lincoln

Rymill and Skelton sit quietly in the captain's cabin, the XO on the single chair and Rymill on the edge of his bed. In the muted light of a bedside lamp Skelton notes small things, an unfolded shirt, a Bible open on the desk.

"Hank, these people are a distraction." Rymill's right hand chops the air, away from his face. "A distraction for the crew, and for me. We've got to stay sharp. Focused on the job."

"Yes, sir. Your orders?"

"Mafri is fine. But this whale scientist, Palmer, has diverted the chief from his job. And that woman." Rymill flicks the Bible closed. "If they want to save the world they will not do it from my boat."

"Sir," Skelton clears his throat, "rescuing these people has been a real boost to morale. And Mafri is excited about this whale research. I would recommend that we let them continue for now."

"What?"

"I'll monitor them, sir. I'll take responsibility. And I think the Navy will need to understand more about what they've found." The XO opens a printout covered with contour lines. "You really should study this map, sir."

The Lincoln's Mess

"Mr. Skelton, do I need an attorney?" Graham asks.

"That won't be necessary, Dr. Palmer. The captain has agreed to release you and your colleagues from your confinement, and to allow you to conduct an initial investigation into your recent discovery."

Hank Skelton has convened a meeting of Chief Mafri and the three scientists in the mess hall.

"You won't be permitted back on the bridge." The XO looks pointedly at Mafri. "But space has been made for you here. The chief has set up your computer and discs. I'll check in from time to time."

"Thank you, sir," Mafri says. "My apologies, sir."

"It's all right, Chief," the XO says, "but you're responsible to see this doesn't affect operations."

"Yes, sir." Mafri turns to Graham. "I'm sorry, Professor. Friends?"

The navy man offers his hand and his apology is so sincere Graham can't refuse.

"It's okay. If not for you, who knows if I'd have made the connection?"

"Great," Kate says. "Let's get started."

≪≪≪

"Looks like the victim of a long-lost battle, alone in an empty sea." Mafri's voice is husky.

"His fate isn't shown," Graham says, "but it's difficult to deny."

The scientists are working on the lexicon and a number of the off-duty men have stopped eating to gather round.

"Who knows how long ago that man died, cold and far from his own?" Mafri touches his dog tags.

"Might've been a merchant marine," a crewman says, "daring the Archangel run against the U-boats."

"Maybe an Armada Spaniard," Brandon Taylor suggests, "defeated more by bad weather and arrogant leaders than by Elizabeth's fleet."

"Whatever his homeland or his purpose," Mafri says, "he was a man of the sea. Any of us might face the same."

Eric clears his throat, and intones:
Like a drop of rain
He sinks into thy depths with bubbling groan
Without a grave
unknell'd, uncoffin'd, and unknown.
A moment of silence holds the room.

The men bring over their personal devices and before long there are a half-dozen teams working in the mess.

Kate's team finds the second image of a human.

"Look at this." She calls the others to join them. "It's a family, a father and mother together at a beach, teaching their little boy how to swim. This one is longer, and you can sense the whale's pleasure at seeing these clumsy creatures paddling."

"You can also sense the whale's shyness," Graham says. "It doesn't want to intrude. But it's like an ultrasound; recording bones, beating hearts, and moving muscles."

"Graham." Kate pauses from cataloguing the entry. "Captain Rymill should see this."

"Not yet," says Graham.

❰❰❰

"Dr. Palmer, I understand from the chief that your lexicon is growing."

Twenty-four hours have passed and Hank Skelton has once again gathered Mafri and the three scientists for a debriefing.

"We've been working from my library of blue whale songs," Graham replies. "I've got hours of recordings on disc. So far it's just a vocabulary of single images. Some are quite clear and concrete."

"Like the krill that the whales depend upon for food," Kate says.

"Yes," Palmer agrees. "But many are still open to interpretation."

"I think there's one of a whale calf in its mother's womb," Eric says.

"And another I'll have to re-label later." Graham looks at Eric.

"You mean the surfer dude," Kate smiles, "labelled 'shark bait'?"

"But on one topic, we all agree," Graham says. "The maps are the find of a lifetime."

"Oh, yes. The maps." Skelton nods.

"Sir," Mafri says, "it's amazing. For all the centuries of sail, we've plumbed the depths with a few hundred yards of cord and a lead sinker. We touched dots here and there like Braille along the margins of the land. Two-thirds of our maps were blank. I remember as a boy seeing the National Geographic undersea maps. I spent hours poring over the seamounts and trenches."

"Me too," Skelton agrees. "That unknown country."

"All the while," Mafri says, "for God knows how long, the whales have been singing these maps to each other."

"So rich in detail." Kate is reverent.

"Not just the contours of the sea bottom and shore," Graham says. "You can see the movement of currents and tides. The effect is mesmerizing."

"But you have to admit," Mafri says, "that what has touched us most deeply is the most familiar — the images of human beings."

"The first one we saw," Graham explains, "was like a video snapshot, only a few seconds long. A single figure treading water, with wreckage floating around him."

"To see ourselves," Kate says, "as another species sees us."

Mafri nods. "You'll remember, Mr. Skelton, the Earthrise photographs? The ones taken by the Apollo astronauts, Christmas Eve, 1968? They show our planet, hanging alone in the darkness of space, above the desolate moon. The Earthrise photos told you that we're alone in the universe. These images say that maybe, just maybe, we're not.

"Sir, we have had an idea," Mafri says.

"An idea?" Skelton eyes them cautiously.

"We could talk to him," Mafri says. "Talk to the blue whale."

"Hold on just a minute. You're suggesting that we transmit . . . whale song?"

"Yes, sir."

"That we deliberately make noise?"

"Yes, sir."

"Mafri, the *Lincoln* lives by keeping silent."

"Commander, we do have a plan," Kate insists.

"Doctor Sexsmith," Skelton says, "you want a boomer to deliberately make noise?"

"The hydrophone will be low-powered and the calls will sound completely natural," says Mafri. "It won't raise any threat to the boat. It'll even disguise our ambient noise. Like camouflage."

"I'm willing to withhold judgment. You explain it to the captain." Skelton's voice is firm. "The lexicon is fascinating and all, but you're not to do anything about this without the captain's permission, understood?"

"Yes, sir."

"In theory, how would it work?" Skelton asks.

Mafri, Kate and Eric look to Graham.

"Well," he says, "in theory, we would take the images from the whales' own songs and piece them together. To make a message."

Skelton looks to Mafri. "Okay, Chief, say we did want to try this, how would you transmit the message?"

"That kind of sound, over that much range," Mafri says, "we'd need a hydrophone transmitter capable of sending high fidelity acoustic signals."

He slides a hand into a paper bag tucked under his chair and produces a compact yellow cone.

"Like this one."

Ring

The past three days have been a time of peace and rest for Ring.

He has allowed the Eastern Current to help him keep up with the Fragment. He has drifted, quietly feeding on krill, and although his jaw still aches from the battle, his mouth is healing.

Once each day and once each night he dives to the base of the ice wall and sends forth the warning. He will continue this task until enough days have passed for the night-sky light to have gone dim and returned to full brightness again. That should give enough warning.

Tonight's moon is a vague circle of light. He tries to call Milk-Eye and the others. There's no reply. The terror has sent them north. When the moon's cycle is over he'll go looking for them.

The creak and grind of the Fragment is unending but the ocean he swims in, behind the giant iceberg, lacks most of the usual sounds of life. He's heard no other whales since the Killer pack's departure. No seal's bark or penguin's squawk. It's restful, but it's boring and lonely.

So when the crazy song comes, it garners his full attention.

It's Blue, but the whale who sings it has lost his mind. The transitions are jagged, absent any glissando, as though the singer has a damaged throat. The order is confused and anti-lyrical.

The gist seems to be "Blues. Swim here." Followed by a sound map of the ocean centred near where he is currently swimming.

The song, if you can call it that, is like baby-talk. It comes from a place near the centre of that map, but a tonal shift tells Ring that the singer is remarkably deep — swimming below the warm/cold water layer, where Blues seldom dive.

He sings a more natural version back in the direction of the crazy Blue to acknowledge the call and adds to the end of the song the ring of bubbles Mother chose as his name.

All right crazy one, he says to himself, I'm coming to see you.

The Lincoln

"It worked!"

Graham stands on a chair and holds his laptop screen up to show everyone the response.

"It's our message repeated back to us. But in a different order, and the transitions are smoother. Then comes the clincher — a ring of air bubbles! Kate has suggested, and I think she's right, that this is the call-sign of a specific, individual whale."

Off-duty crewmen, who now are calling themselves the Whale Study Group fill the mess hall with high-fives and backslaps. Near the door Mafri raises his famous hand and the men settle down.

"First, we have to thank Commander Skelton for helping get the captain's permission for this experiment."

The XO nods in response to an enthusiastic outburst of applause.

"Second, I think our new friend needs a name," the chief says.

"Bubbles!" is the reply from several men at once. The group gives up delighted laughter.

Mafri points. "Kate, I see your hand up."

Kate climbs up on a second chair, next to Graham.

"Names are important," she says. "What you're called affects whether people take you seriously or not. I don't just see bubbles. If his name is Bubbles there wouldn't be any shape to it. This is a circle, a ring. I propose we call him Ring."

"Let's have a show of hands. All in favour?" Mafri's request is met by a forest of arms. "Carried."

"Okay, clear out. Get some rest everyone," Skelton says. "I've got to write a report for the captain. Good work all." He points the crewmen out through the bulkhead door.

"We few, we happy few," Graham murmurs. He remembers the finbacks near Auckland watching the boy he had been.

Do you wish to know me? they had asked.

"I do. I do," he replies.

The Facts

No one part of the Fragment is identical to another.

Its northern rim is a world of chaos. Pack-ice, bulldozed by the Fragment, has been swept up into a bramble, miles deep, piled up and over itself in a frozen explosion. The corpses of countless penguins lie within, broken by the onslaught.

Behind this jumble rises the Wall. A hundred metres above the waterline and six hundred below, the Shelf is old, formed before Columbus stumbled his way across the Atlantic.

In the Fragment's back, imbedded like spears, are vast sections of the four glaciers. Byrd, Nimrod, Beardmore, and Shackleton. Truly ancient, each is a fortress, hard as granite, laminated layer upon layer over the millennia.

Beyond the Ross Sea's rim, the Circumpolar Current lays claim to the Fragment. Giga-joules of power from current, wave, and wind turn it, changing the juggernaut's path from north to east, accelerating it toward the narrow seas of the Drake Passage. An ordinary berg, like the one that gave the *Titanic* a North Atlantic kiss in 1912, might cruise the sea-lanes for months.

There are a variety of physical factors that affect the Fragment.

The first is gravity.

Because of its size it's not really a flat object at all. It actually curves across the surface of the earth, like the last piece of skin to be peeled off an orange.

The second is inertia.

This is basic Newtonian physics. It takes an outside force to change the direction and speed of any object. The greater the mass, the greater the force needed, and the Fragment is a mass like no other.

But Mother Nature deals in immense forces every day. Atlantic hurricanes that release an atom-bomb's worth of energy every minute. Ocean currents that move millions of cubic miles of water every day.

And by leaving the shelter of the Ross Sea, the Fragment finds an outside force truly worthy of her. The Antarctic Circumpolar Current, known to some as The Great Eastern.

At first the following seas build and thrust against the Shelf's western edge, like a tide that's found an unexpected shore.

Thirty metre waves flail against this barrier and the water rises above normal sea level, a metre, two, four, as it pushes inexorably eastward. With each passing hour the current accelerates the Fragment, until its speed matches the current's flow.

Two hundred miles east, across the Fragment's rigid back, at its new leading edge, is a calm and placid sea, the likes of which the Drake Passage has not seen in millennia.

But the sloppy waves of that newly pacific ocean are a false promise. Behind them comes the Wall.

The creatures of the sea meet the Wall in their millions. The air breathers, penguins, seals, dolphins, and so on, have no hope. They swim and die, exhausted and drowned.

For many of the water breathers like fish and squid, the drop in temperature near the Fragment is too much. Sharks, that must move to breathe, slow in the frigid waters until too little water passes over their gills and they asphyxiate. Some species of fish, well able to withstand the cold, succumb instead to the unfamiliar fresh water that has begun to pool around the Fragment.

A lucky handful, the Blues who've heard Ring's strange warning call, save themselves by swimming out of the Fragment's path.

And though Ring's song is harsh-throated, they send it on ahead to warn their kin. They are safe and left to wonder about the first new song that many have heard in their lives.

PART FOUR

The Rose Sayer

"This is Nancy Pepper reporting from the *Rose Sayer* in the South Atlantic."

Langford looks at the petite reporter, noting her Goth-black hair and her orthodontist's dream-smile. Her cameraman, Ben Irons, captures it all in a classic one-third/two-thirds frame, while the chopper that delivered them lifts off behind her.

"That's in the can," Ben says, and shuts down his video camera, turning to the job of carrying their belongings downstairs.

Like many cameramen Langford's met, Ben Irons is built on a large scale. At least six foot three and three hundred pounds, he has the bulk to wear the steady-cam rig, batteries, and equipment belt like fashion accessories and the strength to heft all that gear, including a satellite uplink and Nancy's makeup trunk.

"Stop, stop. Ben, Ben, Ben," Langford says. "Let the stewards look after all that. You and Nancy are my guests. Let me show you around. Help you get settled in. You must be starving."

"Thanks, Mr. Langford, I'll just follow my nose. Nancy, my pager is on." He leaves everything behind for the white-starched boys, and heads below.

Nancy Pepper looks ambitious and intrigued. Langford knows his reputation as a rainmaker has spread among her colleagues. On three previous occasions he's dropped reporters into the middle of a decent story. This one wants more. A story that will get her noticed.

Well, it's unlikely another ship will appear in this empty ocean. They aren't within a thousand miles of anywhere anyone actually cares about. Time will tell.

Forest is cautiously optimistic. Robert Bell Jr. has shanghaied him, but he has a new plan. Play this right and he'll be the new public face of White Star Lines; he'll be more powerful than Chrysler's Lee Iacocca or Wendy's Dave Graham. That will give him leverage with the Mandarins. But right now there's this cute little reporter.

"Nancy," he says, "are you hungry?"

"You're sure this mystery event of yours is going to be an exclusive?" she asks.

"Who knows? What can I tell you? Just kidding. It's one-hundred-percent guaranteed. You see anyone else out here?" His gesture spans the empty horizon. "Miss Pepper, in forty-eight hours you're going to have the story of a lifetime."

The Lincoln

Graham and the other two scientists have hardly left the mess since making first contact. Their early attempts at whale-speech are clumsy, but with suggestions from Mafri and the rest, they've made real progress. It doesn't hurt that Ring is an excellent teacher.

"He wants to know our name," Graham comments.

"What do you mean?" asks Eric.

"See, originally he included the bubble ring about every fifth message. Now it's at the end of every one. See?"

"You're right," Kate agrees, "Ring's being subtle about how rude we've been. He's saying *'This is my name. What's yours?'*"

"Suggestions?"

"I can't think of anything in the database that's going to resemble Abe Lincoln," Eric says.

"How about Nautilus?" Graham calls up a sonar picture of a Nautilus squid on the computer screen.

"Nice choice, Captain Nemo." Kate squeezes his shoulder.

"Or are you thinking of Robert Fulton's submarine?" Eric asks.

"Why not both?" Graham says.

With a mouse-click he tells the computer to add the image to the end of every outgoing message, like the automatic signature on his email account.

"Nemo or Fulton," Kate says, "I think Mafri and the crew will approve."

The Marcy

"Ta dum, ta dum, something, something of the Queeeeen's Navy. Of the Queeeeeeen's Naaaavy . . . ".

Jay Traljesic is alone on deck, singing tunelessly to himself.

"Good thing you don't have to sing for your supper, lad," was Blair Cockburn's earlier assessment.

It's Jay's turn at the helm while Al and Cockburn sleep. They're all exhausted from days of cold, wind, and water.

They're still in the lee of the Fragment. Though they've not yet seen it, it has to be close, running toward them on the powerful easterly current, while Jay holds their course south by southwest.

This lee sea is sloppy. The waves surge awkwardly, as though they remember power and resent the loss. They aren't the huge waves they saw earlier. These eddy and suck at the keel, pitching the deck at odd angles, making it tough to maintain his feet, let alone a decent heading.

Jay battles eyelids heavy with sleep. An hour ago he was able to see the stumbling rollers and make allowance for them. Now grey condenses out of the moist salt air and he has lost any chance of anticipating their erratic rush.

Visibility drops. The fog thickens in arcs, driven ahead by cold air, heavy with the tang of iodine. To starboard a table-sized slab of ice floats out of the grey and is gone before he can react.

"Ice. Not good."

He wants to call Cockburn on deck, but hesitates. It's just a little piece and he hasn't hit it. No reason to get jumpy. The man needs his rest. He'll hold off a while longer and let them sleep. To be safe he lets wind spill from the *Marcy*'s sails to reduce their speed, and rocks with the sloop's wallowing gait. He squints ahead, hoping for a break in the whitening glare.

"Uh-oh."

With one hand he thrusts the tiller, throwing the helm hard to port and cranks madly with the other to raise the weighted keel, desperate to let the *Marcy* side-slip abeam the wind.

Out of the glare comes sound, and shape, and mass.

The sound is from curling waves that seethe past the thing to meet in a turbulent reunion.

The shape is god-like, a rough-hewn avatar in star-cracked white and blue.

The mass is undeniable. Given the chance, this thing would swat the *Marcy* out of existence.

It's only an iceberg. An impatient outrider that has calved and run ahead of the Fragment.

Thankfully this lesser god has no patience for the chase and lets Jay's clumsy maneuver slip the *Marcy* past un-holed. Un-holed, but not untouched.

Intense cold falls from the berg's shoulders, through the fog, across the little sloop's deck, riming him and the vessel in layers of frost. Ice crystals appear on the mast, stays and sheets. They make over the deck in opals and cover his clothes in an armored skin.

He draws breath and the frozen air bites his throat.

Gasping, he hauls open the cabin door and falls forward, shedding hoarfrost over Al and Cockburn as they struggle to escape their salt-grimed sleep.

Ring

Call and answer. Call and answer.

Ring follows the stranger's voice toward a rendezvous. The longer they speak to each other the more curious things are becoming.

Why is the voice at times familiar, and at times foreign? Half the time it sounds female. The melodies are always odd and unconventional and the stranger never uses the same song twice.

They began as simple as a newborn's. But now the constant re-combination of old song elements makes him think about the creative Blues who lived before the Slaughter. To find someone like that would make everything he's gone through worth the cost.

The stranger doesn't seem to have a name — none of his songs end with a signature. Ring adds his own name to the end of each call, just to see if the stranger will do the same.

At first nothing changes. Then a new image appears at the end of each call. It's a signature he would never expect a Blue to use.

It's a spiral-shelled squid. Not food. Generally ignored by his family. Still, it's appealing and distinctive.

The Rose Sayer

"Collins, my timeline is critical."

Forest Langford is in the captain's day cabin, next to the *Rose Sayer*'s bridge. Behind him is the operations deck where the shift officers monitor navigation and handle the ship.

"Some days," says Collins, "the true challenge is to refrain from throttling the little beggars that come through the bridge on the behind-the-scenes tour. The concept of 'don't touch' is foreign to so many children that I've had that junior captain's station installed." He points at a half-height control panel near the cantilevered front windows. "It has a wheel and plenty of toggles and buttons to keep them occupied. One is marked 'Sink Ship'. The number of times that's been pushed — well, it makes you wonder at the future of the human race."

Langford gets up and paces the room. He has no time for this.

"What's your maximum speed?"

"I don't think — "

"Maximum speed, Captain!"

"Mr. Langford, the sea state dictates our maximum speed. Currently, we've got an eight foot swell. Our speed of fourteen knots allows us to make good progress, while at the same time avoiding ship-to-wave harmonics that can cause seasickness in the passengers."

"Forget the passengers."

"The *Rose Sayer* can make thirty knots if one doesn't care about — "

"Thirty knots it is, then."

"You don't understand, sir — "

"No, you don't understand, Captain. I don't give a shit about the passengers. As far as you're concerned, there are only three important people on board this ship, the CNN reporter, her cameraman, and me. I've promised her a big story within forty-eight hours and we, Captain, are going to deliver. The rest of your passengers can puke their guts up for all I care."

"You don't have the authority — "

"No, I don't. You do. But I can recommend that you be assigned to another ship. Maybe that mouldy little river cruiser we have on the Amazon?"

Collins holds his tongue. He picks up the handset from his desk and speaks to the helm. "Make flank speed, Mr. King."

Within seconds the order is relayed. The *Rose Sayer* throws herself ahead and the deck begins to tremble. Her prow cuts the eight-foot swell like a dulled axe. Spray drenches the forward observation deck and stewards scurry to escort passengers aft and clear away the deck chairs.

"Thank you, Captain." Langford says. He leaves quickly, not wanting Collins to see his sudden discomfort.

"Wait till you see the Drake, Mr. Langford," Collins calls behind him.

Ring

Ring swims at the surface, resting and feeding a safe distance from the Fragment's western cliffs.

Nautilus' voice still comes from the depths.

Ring can't understand this.

126

The stranger hasn't risen for hours.

Not even sperm whales stay down that long.

Ring sounds the sonar shape of every species he knows at the stranger.

What kind of being are you?

Silence. Then the deep reply.

It is brief — a combination of two symbols.

Humans / a Ship.

The Lincoln

"What's he going to make of that, Graham?" Kate asks.

Till now, she has kept out of it while the Maori and the big Australian engaged in a sharp argument over how to answer Ring's query about what they are.

"I still think it will frighten him away," Eric says. "That's my assessment. I've no illusions about the relationship between humans and cetaceans. The image of a harpooned blue whale in the first translated message is going to remain with me for a long time."

"I'm not going to lie." Graham is adamant. "This is first contact. Do you want Ring to lie to us? The truth, no matter how ugly, has to be the bedrock of communication with another species. Any other choice would be immoral and unscientific."

She thinks Graham might take a swing at the Australian, but Eric holds his hands out in surrender and steps away from the console.

"Okay, you're the expert," he says.

"You know, Graham. Eric isn't wrong. What do we say? *Pleased to meet you. By the way, my people kill your people for dog food. Care to chat about it?*" Her voice is full of loathing for human cruelty. "Not a start on the right foot, is it?" She turns her face away.

Graham looks at the space between them.

"You're both right. But we're scientists. If we're going to change that equation we've got to do it with the truth."

Neither she nor Eric can dissuade him. Neither tries very hard. They've all seen the factory ships that ply the Antarctic waters. Seen them and done nothing to stop the hunt.

If Ring is going to trust them, they will have to be truthful.

The Marcy

"Maybe we should turn back."

Jay lies in a cold, sodden bunk. He hears Al's lowered voice through a mist of pain. The cabin is dark, hiding the chaos that comes of three men living for days in a confined space. Damp shirts and socks hang on jerry-rigged lines and wait for dry air that will never find its way in here. The floor is littered with wet boots and bags of garbage that Cockburn insists they will take back to port.

"On the Marcy, we don't drop our crap overboard."

"If you want to go home, we'll go home," Cockburn replies to Al. The Scotsman's tone is flat with disappointment. "It's your charter."

Jay wants to object but the railway spike in his larynx sidelines that idea. The inside of his throat is raw meat.

"Yeah," Al says. "Thanks. I'll let you know in a minute."

The hatch door opens; a halo of too-bright light fills the cabin. It closes, leaving Al's silhouette a dark afterimage. Cockburn has gone on deck, leaving them to make up their minds.

"Jay." Al moves closer, steadies himself against the *Marcy*'s cant and sits on the bunk's edge. "Don't talk. Take my hand — one squeeze for yes. Two for no. Okay?"

The clasp says more to Jay about friendship than he's ever known.

"You were on deck. Remember?"

Jay squeezes a yes.

"You got us past an iceberg in the fog. Cockburn said good work by the way — next time, don't cut it so close."

Another squeeze.

"Cockburn thinks you got hit by a katabatic wind. You breathed in some very cold air and it's damaged the membranes in your throat, and maybe your lungs. There were ice crystals in your mouth. I'm worried that it may have harmed your voice."

Emphatic squeeze.

"I think we should get you to a doctor, to prevent anything permanent."

Jay doesn't want to respond. Of course, he wants to say "no, let's go on," but this is his career they are talking about. Without his voice, *his* voice — not some croaky, damaged half-voice — he'll be off I-TV before the lawyers can open their briefcases. The spike in his throat is no joke. He remembers a mouth full of splintered glass.

He squeezes once — for "Yes. Let's go home," and receives his friend's answering, understanding squeeze. Al must recognize his rancor about giving up and probably feels the same.

It isn't losing the story that matters. It's more than that. He and Al have had this one chance — this one chance to be heroes, and it will not come again. They will slink back to Tierra del Fuego, beaten by a fragment of the Fragment, and fly home without ever seeing the monster itself. The taste of ashes will become as familiar in his mouth as household words.

Jay extracts his hand. He needs to get out of this shitty little hole. He needs air, even if it hurts to breathe. He doesn't bother with boots or coveralls, shrugs off the snagging clotheslines, pushes past a surprised Al and goes out the companionway on deck.

Bright sunlight and an iodine wind catch his aching chest, burn his eyes. Tears blur the world. He backhands them away.

Cockburn is in harness, out over the gunwale, leaning hard to counterbalance the sloop's sails. Tiller extension in hand, eyes focused past Jay's shoulder, he holds the course at southwest. The Scotsman is invested in their quest too. Even if Jay could speak, nothing he might say would mean a damn.

A slight shift in the boat's stance tells him that Al has joined them on deck. Jay turns. And then he sees it.

Where Cockburn has been staring, off their starboard bow, is the thing they've come so far to find.

The monster.

The Fragment.

The Wall.

The iceberg they encountered earlier in the fog was god-like, but this is God.

The sun is a brass circle and the Barrier glows with light, within and without.

Now it isn't his throat that hurts, it's his heart. They've made it. They are Ahab fulfilled, and cannot turn from their destiny.

Jay takes Al's hand again, the one he'd rejected moments before, and squeezes. Once. Twice. "No." To answer his friend's last question.

A frown shows Al's confusion and Jay extends his other arm straight at the Wall and squeezes again — a single, unstoppable squeeze — an emphatic "Yes!" to the Fragment — to stay with the great White Wall, no matter what it might cost.

If he, Jay Traljesic, has anything to say about it, today the three of them will be heroes.

The Rose Sayer

From the captain's table, Forest Langford watches passengers fill the main dining room.

The cruise ship's motion isn't pleasant, but that hasn't kept anyone from the all-you-can-eat trough.

His earlier unease has passed and Forest feels like he's starting to get his sea legs. As he expected, the captain's dire warnings are nonsense and he further discounts the man's value.

He sees the CNN reporter and her cameraman take a corner booth near the entrance and decides to leave his guests on their own for now. He's arranged with a maître d' for them to receive white glove service. He wants them happy and pliant.

Meanwhile, in the place next to him, the captain attacks his food with epicurean gusto.

"Quite the life you have here, Captain," Forest says, and orders for himself. "A green salad, no dressing."

When it becomes clear that the captain intends to keep silent, Langford retreats into observation mode.

The captain and his guests are enjoying what White Star calls dynamic dining, a parade of perfect meals. Plates come, bearing artistically arranged food, ready for *Bon Appétit* magazine. Some leave despoiled, consumed save for the parsley sprig survivors, others untouched.

Then, after the fifth course has been served, something changes.

Growing shockwaves tremble both crystal stemware and the salon's picture windows in a restrained, humming resonance. The room buzzes with questions.

Forest's stomach rises and for a moment he imagines how the grand salon might look turned upside down.

The captain looks up from his half-empty plate. "The *Rose Sayer* has passed out of the Horn's lee, Mr. Langford. We have entered the Drake. At the speed you wanted, sir. On the course you've set. The ship strives to meet the worst seas in the worst way. We're matching her horsepower against the sea's power and all bets are off."

This isn't the triumph he expected to feel, to have a ship answering his commands.

The gyrations worsen and the Drake exacts its toll. A plague of nausea falls upon the *Rose Sayer*, as the ship's churning progress touches stomachs full of Chicken Tandoori and Fruit Salad Surprise.

Passengers stream for the exits, many of the men failing to honour the maxim of "Women and children first."

Conditions in the grand salon grow markedly worse as staff members begin to fall ill.

"Allow me to paint you a picture, Langford," Captain Collins says. "Meeting these seas head-on would ameliorate the worst of these effects, but because you insist on this course, west by southwest, the *Rose Sayer* must take the swells at an oblique angle. This adds a reciprocating, elliptical motion — combining port and starboard pitches with forward and stern yaws. Look about you."

Forest is dimly aware of brave stewards leading strike teams deep into motion sickness territory to distribute medication, only to return stained and drained. Nothing has prepared him for this. He wonders if he is going to die. Then he wishes he would.

Soon, only three men remain — Forest, the captain, and a starchly formal maître d'.

With apparent deference the captain says, "You're ill, Mr. Langford. Let Mr. Randolph escort you to your cabin."

"No. If you can take this, I can too."

"Quite right." The captain turns to the maître d'. "Randolph, do bring out the Lobster Thermidor. Sure you won't have some, Mr. Langford?"

"Oh God, no." Forest lurches from the table.

❮❮❮

Forty-eight hours, several naps, and countless visits to the head later, Langford has recovered enough of his brio to finish the damned job.

He is at Nancy Pepper's stateroom door.

"Miss Pepper!" he bellows. "Wake up!" He rattles the door handle and shouts, "Rise and shine! Time to get your exclusive off the blocks."

Faint protests issue from doorways up and down the hall and a miasma of puke wafts past. From inside Nancy's room comes a heartfelt request. "Let me die in peace."

"Not yet I won't," he replies.

After a moment he goes in search of a steward who might have a passkey.

The *Rose Sayer* has slowed and her excellent sea-keeping design is bringing the living dead back from the land of vomit.

During his last time hanging over the deck rail he saw the thing they've come for.

The engine had throttled back, returning the horizon to its accustomed horizontal, the ship's bow had come about and the Fragment loomed in the distance. Forest Langford stared at the temptress wreathed in veils; it teased him with hints of chromatic ecstasy.

"Anticipation." Forest sings softly as he looks for a steward.

He is going to make marketing history and needs Nancy for the garnish.

"Where's a damned steward? I need a passkey!"

Ring

Humans / a Ship.

Nautilus' answer is bizarre.

Humans who talk and sing in strange Blue-like voices? It's hard to swim into but the conclusion is unavoidable. The clumsy little shore paddlers are masters of the slaughtering monsters.

The clues have been waiting for him, hidden in old images.

His father and the other older whales knew, but have chosen not to explain it to Ring's generation. Is to speak of the hunters to summon them?

Ships aren't the killers. Humans are. Pathetic and frail, they use the hard, noisy things to murder Blues and many other kinds of ocean life.

But how could they be so hungry?

Ring shakes with disbelief.

Nautilus seemed stupid at first, but friendly.

Does he want to eat Ring?

If so, why has he waited so long, singing the same things over and over?

Is it all a trick to lure him in closer for the kill?

The Rose Sayer

From the moment Nancy set foot on the *Rose Sayer* little has gone as planned.

Within an hour of reaching the White Star ship, high seas had forced her to retreat into her cabin, where she'd tossed her cookies like a hyperactive bulimic and prayed that this wretched scow would please-God-hit-a-rock-and-just-let-her-die, while it corkscrewed her across a heaving ocean the colour of day-old guacamole.

The only good news out of the two-day forced purge was that she'd dropped to under a hundred pounds for the first time in three years. Take that, Katie Couric!

Then, finally, when the world and her stomach stopped spinning, that lunatic Forest Langford had hauled her sorry ass out of bed, practically kidnapping her, pouring black coffee down her throat.

Of course in the chaos someone's unspeakable vomit had gotten onto the chic designer après ski-wear she'd brought specifically for the cold-weather shots, and the ship's stupid cleaners' rush job had ruined everything.

The only rag from the on-board shop that came close to fitting her was an off-the-rack snow-suit designed expressly to put twenty pounds on her hips.

On top of all that, Langford forced her to work eight straight hours yesterday. She still can't believe it. No one in the biz ever works a story for more than a couple of hours at a time. That's the way TV news works. No story plays for longer than a few minutes, so bagging a few good takes is all you really need. That and a killer smile.

Only the old ladies like Barbara and Connie do the long pieces.

Worst of all, somewhere along the line the natural order of the universe has turned upside down and Ben Irons, the cameraman, has started to give *her* orders.

"Stand here next to the railing. Turn this way, turn that way. Lift your chin more."

As though he's a director or something.

And he insists on more and more takes, changing locations all around the ship. First the helicopter deck, then the bow, the stern, inside the bridge with the captain and crew arranged like mannequins — all at Irons' command, with Langford's tacit approval; and always with the damned iceberg in the background.

Maybe it happened while she was sick. There has been a shift in power and Forest Langford and Ben Irons have suddenly become dictators.

Each time Langford nods his head Ben Irons translates his desires, no matter how outrageous, into action.

The ship's captain, a good-looking older man named Collins, now turns to the White Star VP Langford for approval.

"Closer to the Fragment," Langford says. That's what he and Ben call the big iceberg, "The Fragment," like it's holy or something. "More. Closer. Take us south, along the east side."

"Hurry, this light won't last," Ben Irons says. "Farther south. Faster. There'll be an Aurora tonight. We can't miss that."

And then Ben starts ordering Langford around, too.

"I need that battery pack. Hold this reflector on Nancy. Higher. Good. Steady now."

And the big dork Langford obeys him like he's some go-fer asshole. Nancy's estimation of both of them has gone downhill. Langford's no rainmaker. Ben's a pissant. The captain obeys, though. And, she is embarrassed to admit, she obeys them too. Maybe she's suffering the after-effects of too much Dramamine, but Irons has become King of the World and this is turning into some lame-ass James Cameron fantasy.

Working inside the bridge isn't too bad. It's warm and out of the wind and the guy at radar, Ltn. Duncan, is young and cute in that *An Officer and A Gentleman* crew-cut kind of way. He has nice eyes and she likes the way his mouth moves just a tiny bit when she sheds the Teletubby snowsuit.

Although she feels a teensy bit guilty about this, that maybe he should be watching the radar screen instead of her, because now the shits hit the fan.

Under Grand-Admiral Irons' command, the *Rose Sayer* has threaded her way south beside "the Fragment" through the icebergs that trail it like ducklings following their momma.

There's a couple mile gap between one berg and the next and they are slipping through pretty smoothly.

She is trying to think of a way to use "slipping through" as a witty double-entendre, when Ltn. Duncan glances at the radar screen and stops looking at her entirely.

"Captain. Trouble, sir."

"Report."

Although he's way too old for her, Nancy thinks the captain is pretty cool — like Ian McShane in *Deadwood*, but without all the profanity.

"The edge of the main iceberg off our port bow, sir, it's fractured, calving. Maybe a couple of square miles are breaking up."

The bridge crew crowd around and Nancy is squeezed between broad-shouldered men. From what she can see the radar screen is a mess. It shows one big blob — that must be "the Fragment" — and a shotgun blast of smaller dots radiating outward from it. She slips out of the knot of gold braid and rushes to look out the east windows. Ben Irons is already there, filming.

A semicircle, like a new-made bay, has been torn from the Fragment. Slabs of ice plunge and grandly rise to the surface. Sheets of blue water cascade from their flat-top heads and they shoulder each other in a violent jumble. A stampede of icebergs is headed their way. Nancy's knees go weak. She's no sailor, but from the silence on the bridge, she can tell they're in deep.

She's seen *Titanic* and has no desire to play the Kate Winslet role in real life. Just *one* of those things sank the *Titanic* and now the *Rose Sayer* has bought the Costco giant economy pack.

"Engines full ahead, emergency power, retract the stabilizers." Collins' voice is flat and urgent. Men leap to action and he speaks again over the noise. "Mr. King, note our location and the time in the log along with each of my orders. Helm, steady as she goes."

Nancy glances back at Ltn. Duncan. He looks sick and angry, like he wants to blame her.

"Turn! We've got to turn!" Langford sounds badly frightened.

No one else speaks. Collins gives his back to the White Star VP, looks out the east windows, and straightens his jacket cuffs as though he does this every day. The captain is definitely cool.

"Mr. King, please explain to our guests why we are not turning."

"Yes, sir," King finishes his notation in the log book, working hard to appear as unruffled as his captain. "Mr. Langford, Ms. Pepper, Mr. Irons," he explains, "turning slows the ship. The sharper the turn, the quicker the deceleration. The captain won't trade speed for a change in direction when all that will do is give our stern, the rudder and propellers, to the ice."

"Thank you, Mr. King. Assemble the damage control teams, if you would. I have the bridge."

"Aye, sir." Mr. King plucks a portable radio handset from its cradle and disappears down a stairwell.

Captain Collins is so polite and calm.

Forest Langford, on the other hand, is ash grey.

"Shit, shit." The panic in his voice plucks at the fear in her chest, but she keeps her mouth shut. She's covered enough accident scenes to know how stupid you can sound if you just let your mouth run. Ben's camera mike will pick up everything said in the room and she doesn't intend for posterity to remember her as a fool.

"Nancy," Ben calls softly. His commander-in-chief tone is markedly subdued. "I need you in the shot."

That's great, exactly what she wants to avoid. The big jerk's request is on tape and refusal is not an option. If she doesn't step up, someone, most likely that little bitch Kailee back at the office, will get their hands on it and make her look unprofessional. Nancy would die before she'd look unprofessional on camera.

"Right," she says. Short words are good. You just spit them out. They're too short to carry the nervous quake that haunts

139

her diaphragm. She slides forward, afraid to lift her feet from the deck. She aches to feel the ship's pulse quicken as engines turn more power into more speed. Come on boat. Come on. Go, goddamn it, go.

Ben takes a step back and she is in the frame, there to give human perspective to something inhuman and uncaring. She forces a dry smile, tight lips near ready to split from cold and tension. She looks into the lens.

"This is Nancy Pepper on the *Rose Sayer*. Behind me is the Fragment." She mentally kicks herself. Ben has her doing it too. "A huge ice sheet that has broken off from Antarctica."

It would be standard practice at this point to look back over her shoulder at the object of the report. She dares not. Her composure is tissue thin, not to be tested. She continues, her focus narrowed to the little glass lens. She explains the situation in short staccato bursts, and keeps things simple, both for herself and for the Joe-six-pack audience who might see this someday, assuming she and the crew don't all die in the next few minutes.

The soles of her feet tingle. A changed vibration? Some hint of escape? She fears the shock of impact, the tilt of the deck as it tips backward into oblivion, and she chances a glance at the captain and instantly regrets the impulse. His eyes are pinched with anticipated pain. Hope and dread play across his face, a shifting tide.

"Hard left rudder," he says.

The tone of the order means something is close. The boat turning its ass must mean something's very close.

When the collision comes, it's hardly noticeable. A bang. That's it.

Nancy thinks, "That's all?" and turns, expecting a little ice-flow has glanced off the stern. Instead, a dripping white monster hovers over the ship's rear end. It drops translucent shards onto the open decks like rotten teeth. They explode. Crystalline shrapnel tinkles against twisted metal railings.

Now the orders come fast and furious.

"Port full stop. Starboard ahead full."

The monster has kissed the *Rose Sayer* and Collins is struggling to tear his lady from its embrace.

"Aye, sir." A large brass lever is thrown back. A bell rings.

"Tell Mr. King I need a report from below the water line. Port quarter."

"Aye, sir."

Then Ben touches her elbow.

"Come on," he says.

Ben Irons is gone down the same stairwell Mr. King took, bouncing off the walls, a human cannonball.

The Lincoln

In the *Lincoln*'s mess hall the monitors are blank and the speakers are silent. Graham, Kate, Eric, and the group of crewmen wait, afraid to lose this fragile link.

"Come on," Eric prays. "Don't give up on us."

"How long has it been?" Graham asks.

"Almost an hour," Kate says.

"Maybe we should — " Graham starts.

"No," Kate interrupts. "Like you said, we wait. Have faith."

Long minutes pass. The cooks hand out sandwiches and Graham forces himself to eat.

"Time to stir the blood," Mafri stands and gets them all up for some impromptu calisthenics.

In mid-squat the speakers rumble and a message appears. Graham bolts to his station and sits transfixed.

Nautilus is a human. Nautilus is in a ship.

Kate and Eric go to their computer stations.

"My God." Eric tugs at his beard.

"What now, Graham?" Kate's look is expectant.

"We've got to tell him everything." Graham hesitates over his keyboard. "Explain."

"How?" Eric asks. "What?"

"Who we are." Graham wishes he sounded more certain. "What we've done."

"You mean humanity?" Kate pauses. "You want to explain humans to a whale?"

"I don't think," Eric shakes his head, "I could explain humans to another human."

"He has acknowledged what we are. Humans in a ship," says Graham. "He must know that humans drive the ships that hunt his people. And all that implies."

"So, you think he's giving us a chance to explain?" Kate asks.

"And he wants to know why he shouldn't just turn his back on us," Eric adds.

"That's a tall order." Mafri sounds doubtful. "The lexicon is good, as far as it goes, but so much is missing. How do you convey human ideas like history, nations, or law?"

"Ring has no words for what you want to tell him, Graham." Eric's tone is skeptical.

"Then we have to invent them," Kate says.

No one disagrees.

"We've seen some of the things blues can do," Mafri offers. "Like adding little whale figures to their sonar maps."

"Or morphing the image of a blue into a krill," Graham agrees. "Like in that first song you showed me."

"Right," says Kate. "So they do use abstraction."

"And metaphors," Mafri says. "So 'this is like this' won't be an alien concept."

"That's a good avenue." Graham nods at the chief. "Mafri, can you lead a group to make as many useful image transformations as you can think of?"

"You mean shifts that can convey an idea." Mafri points at a couple of his crewmen, gesturing for them to get started. "Like morphing a hard-shelled crab to jellyfish, to get across the idea of 'soft' or 'soften'?"

Kate nods. "Using the strongest characteristic of the two things."

"Just as Ring did to show the relative size of the Fragment," Mafri adds.

"Exactly. And in reverse, 'jellyfish-to-crab' could work for 'hard' or 'harden'," Graham says.

"A storm that becomes placid could symbolize 'calm' or 'peace'," Eric says.

"Wait a second." Kate gestures for quiet. "Some of Ring's images are clips of action or movement. But they always move forward in time."

"Yes," Graham says, "that's just the way a whale would perceive them happening."

"But what if we ran a clip in reverse?" Kate continues. "There are ideas — "

"Like 'one step forward, two steps back'," Eric says.

"Right. By changing the time direction, running a clip in reverse, or by speeding up or slowing down an action we can create ideas I think Ring will be able to grasp, once we show them to him."

"And he can help us," Graham says. "I'm sure of it."

"He's already taught us most of what we know of Bluish," Eric says.

"Bluish," Mafri laughs. "I like that."

The group shares a smile and Brandon Taylor breaks in. "So, you're just going to ignore the Prime Directive?"

"What do you mean?" Graham knows the reference but wants to hear what the sonarman has to say.

"You're proposing that we build a whole a new layer to blue language. We're used to lots of change. What's this going to do to their culture?"

"I don't see an alternative," Graham says. "If people are going to take blues seriously, they're going to need this. Just to defend themselves."

"You think this is like European contact with — "

"With everybody else. My people, Australian Aborigines, Inuit, Aztecs, Native Americans. Everybody. Do you see?"

"That's true," Eric says. "If you don't even know what the other guy is talking about, private property, ownership of territory — you're screwed."

"Exactly," Graham turns. "Kate, can you take your 'time-shift' idea and run with it?"

She nods. "I see Eric's got an idea, too."

The astronomer smiles. "I do. Let me work on it a bit and I'll get back to you."

《《《

"Okay, everyone," Graham calls the sailors and scientists to attention. "Eric. This is your show. What's your surprise?"

"I've had a lot of help from Brandon Taylor," Eric says. "Like the man said in *Stranger in a Strange Land*, we grok."

The young sailor smiles and flashes a Vulcan hand signal at Mafri. "Watch this, Chief, you're gonna love it!"

Throughout the room the linked computer screens display the same image. It is a still picture of one of the beautifully

144

intricate whale sonar maps showing a portion of the Pacific Ocean floor, centred on a chain of seamounts.

The observer moves toward the broad base of a submarine mountain, then rises through countless fathoms of water. The mountain is cone-shaped and narrows as the view approaches the surface like a fast swimming whale.

But it doesn't stop there. At the surface it leaps higher, hundreds of feet into the air.

The topographical features of an island have been layered onto the whale's underwater map, and a collective gasp is drawn from the viewers. The shoreline, the wrinkled hills and sharp valleys, the roads, Diamond Head, the city of Honolulu, and even the ships of Pearl Harbour appear as though a blue is flying above the surface, taking aerial pictures of the human world.

It is the Hawaiian island of Oahu.

Kate is impressed. "Ring will be thrilled."

"I know, right?" Brandon Taylor is grinning.

The rate of rise increases. The sub-surface details remain, the ocean floor spreading wide to give context to location and scale. The Hawaiian Islands shrink in size to a tiny broken comma of land, and on the edge of the map the continents begin to appear.

Mountains, plains, rivers, and lakes spread across the screen, the elevation lines of human maps converted into the sonar language of the blue whales.

The voice of Andy Trip, the Prowler pilot who spotted the scientists so long ago, comes from Mafri's group, quoting Magee's *High Flight,* "I have slipped the surly bonds of earth," the young airman says, "and danced the skies on laughter-silvered wings."

The vertical ascent accelerates again, like a rocket ship rising to escape gravity's ceaseless pull and now it's the world, the globe, Earth, hanging in space, slowly rotating with subtle clues to indicate the shifting of day into night. The earth shrinks to the size of an orange and is joined by a companion sphere, much smaller, its surface a mosaic of circles laid and overlaid in beautiful contrast to the earth's fractal surface of coastlines and mountain chains; one orb shaped by the shifting forces of plate tectonics, the other by plunging comets and asteroids.

Then a bright dot appears on the surface of the planet and separates itself, headed for the moon. A brief zoom and jump-cut show Ring's images of — *Nautilus is a human. Nautilus is in a ship* — identifying the dot metaphorically with the history of human spaceflight.

The dot circles the plum-sized moon. Then lands.

Eric and Brandon bow to the enthusiastic applause of their peers.

❬❬❬

The teams find inspiration in a wide field of human thought. The languages of photography, film, music, and art all lend their ideas and approaches.

The copy and paste of computer-aided drafting multiplies a drowning man by a thousand, to convey the idea of death on a large scale — as necessary an image for talking about human history as any that Graham can think of.

Ring's images are over-layered, flipped, and zoomed. Parts are erased to emphasize some feature.

Ring

Ring is intrigued, and offers Nautilus what guidance he can.

He draws from Blue history and shares the full song of Long-Throat and the Smoking Mountains. Nautilus sings it back encapsulated and shortened into a split-second representation of *hope*.

He teaches Nautilus Blue syntax and grammar, making images that rotate, rise, or fall, adding nuance to nuance, meaning to meaning.

Nautilus sends an image of Milk-Eye upside down and Ring feels amusement tickling his throat.

But one invention — the "reversal-of-time" — completely stuns him.

He calls for a respite and goes silent while he swims through those utterly alien waters for hours. Nautilus has opened thousands of possibilities.

They sing together for days on end and he understands more. New levels of thought open, and the revision of ancient stories becomes possible.

Nautilus produces model cubes, cones, cylinders, and spheres, and teaches him numbers in the exotic and yet somehow familiar base of ten.

Ring feels the proto-finger bones within his forefins and finds he can count.

The Lincoln

Graham knows the full development and understanding of Bluish, for humans and blues, will take many years, perhaps his entire lifetime.

But now he hopes he has enough to attempt the task that started all of this. He has worked all his life for this kind of breakthrough and he can't bear the thought that his efforts might let others exploit or destroy the creatures he loves.

He asks for Ring's attention to what will be a long and troubling song.

His hands fly from keyboard to mouse, parsing whale-speech concepts, to try and convey human ideas of nations and laws, of power and exploitation.

Kate, Eric, Mafri, and the crewmen make suggestions. Their thinking seems to him more and more unified as the hours pass. Cooks bring them food and drink and are drawn into the maelstrom of explanation.

The boat quickens with excitement as crewmen run down the corridors, skipping through the bulkhead doors with additional reference books. Others burst in with passages from favourite authors, each reaching for the elusive mystery — how to explain to Ring what it is to be human.

And what blues must know, if they are to deal wisely with humans.

Graham's message is clear. There are things to be admired about these fallen angels, but there is far more that Ring and his people must be wary of.

He is robbing the blues of their innocence, but fears more what this sea-bound race would face in a world of seven billion human beings without the knowledge he is sharing with them.

Mafri is his unstinting partner through it all. The chief fields questions and supervises the constantly changing work groups to condense and feed translated information, which the sonarman reviews with Eric and Kate and makes ready for transmission.

Graham tells Ring how nations can be different from one another, that some are whale-killers, some not, or at least, not now, not any longer.

When the long message is finished Ring signals that he will need time to make sense of it all. The screens go blank and the speakers are silent again.

Graham says good night to the other Scott Base survivors.

"Whatever Ring thinks of humanity now," Kate says, "you've done your best. What will happen next is up to him."

He goes to his bunk exhausted. Others will monitor the system and call him back, if necessary.

He lies quietly, facing a previously unrecognized isolation. But he is also joyful for the chance to be here, alive at this moment.

Ring

Resting his voice and listening to Nautilus' long song has brought some relief to the pain inside his damaged mouth, but Ring's head is swimming.

Nautilus has talked through the night and although its world view is strange, Ring senses only kindness, like a mother uplifting her calf. Whatever other humans have done, this one, he feels, can be trusted.

Nautilus has confessed that humans committed the Great Slaughter. Roving the sea as ravenous Killers, they butchered Blues and other whales for their meat and oil. And though a few of the human pods still do this, most have stopped.

Nautilus has explained so many things about the human world.

Some are horrible, beyond belief.

Humans kill their own kind. And not just accidentally or occasionally, but in krill-swarm numbers. He wanted to stop listening, but hearing the difficult truths made it possible to believe the wonders.

Some are just too delightful to believe — humans in a ship have swum to the round night-sky light.

Though there's much to digest, one shining fact stands out above the rest.

Nautilus has promised that when other humans learn whale-talk, the killing will stop.

Ring feels like a newborn. This one unlooked-for hope is worth any risk, any pain he might suffer.

Like Nautilus, he too needs sleep. The Eastern Current carries him along in the penumbra of the Fragment, surrounded by the flotilla of icebergs that trail it. One-half of his brain drifts into sleep, the other imagines a future free from fear.

The Lincoln

Hank Skelton's bed is unmade.

He's had little time for rest. On top of his duties as XO, he has spent hours poring over the translated recordings made by Graham Palmer and his whale gang.

An honest-to-God whale has started talking back. He is hooked by the possibilities. And most importantly the sonar communication doesn't appear to have exposed the boat to any outside threat. At least, not so far.

It's the whale's sonar maps that garner his deepest admiration. On the scientists' monitors they are beautiful, and they are scalable to an incredible degree. He can zoom in again and again, each time finding yet more detailed information.

It's on one of these zoom-quests that he finds the "easter egg".

He takes the discovery to Rymill.

The Rose Sayer

Nancy Pepper is past hesitation.

She clatters behind Ben Irons down the narrow steel stairs. Down, past pinch-faced passengers struggling with life-jacket straps. Past stewards waving emergency phones, their own flooding panic palpable.

"Gangway!" Ben shouts and uses his bulk to batter through the upward surge of bodies.

Nancy grips the back of his shirt and trails in his lee. Then they're past the press of people and in unfamiliar territory, the ship's mechanical spaces, the great lady's guts.

She senses they are below the waterline and the thought is a knife drawn across her windpipe.

"Stop, stop!" She pulls at Ben's shirt back, the damp denim bunched in her fists. The hungry ocean is outside these walls, these thin, crumpled steel walls, and she feels suddenly small and vulnerable. "Ben, I want to go back up. Up like all the others."

Ben does stop. But it isn't her protests that have brought the big cameraman to a halt. It's the steel bulkhead door that blocks their path. It's one of those oval-shaped water-tight doors, the type she's seen in movies, heavy and industrial, complete with steel wheel and lever locks.

Above the lock mechanism is a small round window, and in the window air and water battle.

The elements bisect the glass circle, light and air above, dark and water below. The glass is half full, or half empty, according to your level of optimism.

For a moment they stand, Ben's camera for once held askew, while the smells of hot oil and sweat coat the inside of her throat. Beyond this door the flood is easily five feet deep and condensation beads their side of the glass and steel.

Shadowy figures struggle in the alien world beyond the door. Their purpose is obscure, but none come close to the window, none try to open the door to escape. With her bare hand she wipes cold condensation from the glass. Now she can see.

Men dive below the choppy surface, disappear for long moments, and burst up again for air. A flash of gold catches her eye. She recognizes the captain's man, Mr. King, among them.

"Damage control," she says, not certain what she means by it. Those men inside there, caged with the hungry ocean, are fighting to save the ship, to save *her*.

She steps forward and pokes Ben Irons in the chest with a stiffened forefinger.

"Film me," she tells him.

The camera snaps into place, his ocular appendage, and she speaks.

"Behind me are brave men. We've been hit by a monster. Water is coming in. On the other side of this door you can see Mr. King and his men working to save the ship. Our fate is in their hands."

Irons steps closer to the window, to capture something comprehensible out of the chaos.

"The water is getting higher," Nancy says. "Only a few inches of air still remain. The men are moving more slowly, the terrible cold saps their warmth. As you see, all save one are standing still. They wait, perhaps for the end.

"There is still one man, struggling to make some unseen connection."

The lights beyond the door flicker and die. Silence, then a coughing hum as something electrical catches its breath and begins to whirl. Vibration, strong and real, trembles the metal.

"A pump. A pump!" Nancy cries. Again she swipes clean the window and this time holds a finger up to mark the water level. "A pump is running. Will it be enough to match the incoming flood?"

She wants to unlock the door and let those poor men out. But she needs to keep reporting. "The ocean wants in, to fill every space that engineers and steel have denied it, to fill our lungs, to take our lives. If I were to open this door, they couldn't hope to reseal it again against the weight of the ocean."

Fear stops her voice.

Inside the chamber a flashlight flickers and she can see the partly submerged men huddle together against the brutal cold, slumped against their fellows, as hypothermia steals their strength and purpose.

The Lincoln

"Captain, this is one of the whale sonar maps."

The XO stabs at the screen. As in all of the whale-made charts, multi-coloured lines show in incredible detail the peaks, valleys, and plains of the ocean depths, along with the layers of currents and counter-currents that weave across them.

But Clint Rymill and Hank Skelton stare at something that is *not* there. On this chart, in one tiny area, the lines abruptly break and then reappear. It's a blank. Some small anomaly that the whales could not make sense of, and so have left unfilled.

Skelton and Rymill know what it represents. A boomer. Not the image of a boomer, but the image of its absence.

"I've checked," says Skelton. "That's us. That's the *Lincoln*'s precise position from four days ago, when Mafri recorded this."

"Let me see if I have this straight," Rymill says. "You're saying that the *Lincoln*'s anechoic coating prevents the whales from detecting us. But when it — what, compiles a map inside its head? — it displays our position as empty space?"

"Yes, sir," The XO says. "No computer program in the world could duplicate this. It's like the way people can see details no machine can detect. Not because our eyes are better, but because our brains are better."

"Jesus," Rymill says. "If this gets out . . . "

Skelton sees beads of sweat on the captain's forehead and passes a hand across his own. It comes away with a sour slick. "I think the rewards of communicating with this blue whale outweigh the danger of attracting unwanted attention," he says.

"Hank, this is above our pay grade." Rymill slips on his jacket. "Call Command on the *SSIXS* voice and data link. I want to be able to lay this all out for the admiral."

"Aye, sir."

He has never seen his skipper like this. He sees a man who has lost something precious but has no time to look for it. The whole ballistic submarine program is at risk. Anyone who can read these whale-charts will see in real time where the fourteen American boomers are hiding.

That means the subs would no longer be safe against a first strike. An enemy could take them out far more easily than the concrete missile silos buried in Nebraska. The compression wave from a strategically placed atomic warhead detonated below the surface of the ocean would smash any sub crew within miles into strawberry jam. Fourteen hits would eliminate America's second strike capability and turn the ace in the hole into a deuce at the bottom of the ocean.

Though Rymill would never acknowledge it, this map in the wrong hands would end his career, his command, his way of life.

The congressional bean-counters will understand that if the boomer fleet cannot hide, there's no reason to put the subs out to sea. They may as well sit in port, tied to a dock, with no need for a captain and crew. A few techs can keep the missiles ready and the country would save billions.

And the *Lincoln* will die as a vessel. Rymill's command will be over. Both their careers will be over.

Unbidden, in Hank Skelton's heart an unexpected spark appears.

If all this is true, if all this comes to be, he'll be released from the waking nightmare of "Launch on Command."

Skelton doesn't speak of this to Rymill. They are both warriors and the first thing any warrior must conquer is himself.

The Pentagon — Washington, DC

"Oh, dear. Oh, dear."

Shirley McCall wants to go home. Or anywhere really. So long as it isn't here.

The admiral has been arrested. Shirley saw it all on TV.

And five sharp-suited men are dissecting the admiral's office. She's been instructed to sit down and shut up.

Filing cabinets have already been taped closed and taken away on hand-trucks. The admiral's computer is to be broken down and boxed up too.

Then a sixth man arrives and starts to ask her questions.

He puts Shirley in mind of one of those awful dogs that are always in the news for biting people. The clench of his jaw says that she is just a tiny morsel, and what he really wants to sink his teeth into is the admiral.

The authoritative *whirr* of her telephone is a life saver. She looks at the nasty little man for permission to answer the call.

He stabs the speaker button himself, the pudgy finger showing off a Harvard class ring.

"Hel . . . Hello?" Shirley's automatic routine is flummoxed. "Admiral Hart's . . . I mean, um . . . hello?"

"Shirley, it's June down in Communications. There's a message for the admiral."

"Um, why don't you just send it up, June?"

"I'm sorry, Shirley. I've never had one of these before. It's not text. It's live, voice and data encoded through *SSIXS*. From the *Lincoln*, if you can believe that? Can I patch them through to his desk?"

The bulldog man moves in and Shirley retreats.

"This is Norman Butchart. I think you know who I am, June, honey?" His drawl is thick. "The admiral is, shall we say, finished? I'll take that call. Just do what I tell you, you hear?"

Shirley stays out of the way. She doesn't want Butchart to talk to her like that, ever.

"Get down here, lads, the both of you."

Blair Cockburn's command rises from the dripping twilight of the *Marcy*'s cabin, like the spectre of a dead Scottish king. Jay and Al stoop through the gangway door and hear a crackly voice, less ghostly, but more dire.

"Calling all ships. This is the passenger liner, *Rose Sayer*. We request assistance. Location sixty-three degrees, fourteen minutes south. Eighty-five degrees, eight minutes west. We've been struck by an iceberg. The hull's been holed below the Plimsoll line and we're taking on water. Over."

The voice, American by the sound of it, stops for several long anxious seconds. No reply comes, and the message is repeated.

Cockburn is hunched over his chart table, portable GPS in one hand, grease pencil in the other.

"They're close." He nods at the radio.

Al unclips the handset, clears his throat. "*Rose Sayer*, this is the sloop, *Marcy IV*. We hear you. Over."

"Acknowledged, *Marcy IV*. Request you relay our distress call. Yours is the only reply received so far. Over."

Al looks at Cockburn for direction and the Scotsman shakes his head.

"They think we're a south-seas cruiser, hundreds of miles to the north," he says. "But my radio won't cast a shadow next to the gear they'll have aboard. If they can't be heard, as sure as God made little blue bairns, we can't either." Cockburn hooks a thumb at Al. "Milliken, reef sails and start the engine. Make for zero degrees true north, full speed. We're not more than a few leagues south of that liner. Mind, a sharp eye." And then he turns to Jay. "Give us a hand."

The Scotsman scrounges through a pair of jumbled compartments, hands up a bundle of cork floats, a length of chain, and an old spinnaker. Then he sketches out the plan.

"You get the idea, Jay-lad?"

Jay nods and sets to work with a spool of cord and a marline spike.

Cockburn keys the radio mike.

"This is master of the *Marcy*. Let me speak with your captain."

Twenty minutes later all hands are on the *Marcy*'s deck, Cockburn at the tiller.

"Steady, lads!" Cockburn's bellow echoes off a rutted steel cliff that leans drunkenly over them, his voice pitched to pierce a rising wind.

The *Marcy*'s sails have all been furled, but Jay and Al, their flying harnesses straining, stand out fore and aft, far over the sloop's starboard side. Between them swings the folded bundle of Dacron sailcloth that Jay has prepared. Loose corners buzz in the wind and it threatens to blossom prematurely.

A dozen metres away the battered hull of an ocean liner, the *Rose Sayer*, slides past.

The sight of waves slopping against the liner's crumpled side is sickening, like a parade of parasites come to feast on an open wound. A hundred square metres of the *Rose Sayer*'s hull is folded inward. God only knows what has prevented complete disaster. Hidden among all that wrinkled steel must be the hull breach eager to fill the *Rose Sayer*'s guts.

A reciprocal jet, ice cold, arcs out over the *Marcy*, to show that somewhere inside the *Rose Sayer* a pump strives valiantly against the incoming flood.

"On my mark!" Cockburn calls.

He means to bring the *Marcy* close enough for the hole's own suction to pull the temporary patch into place. Too far away and the patch may be lost. Too close and a wave will crack the little sloop against the big liner like a walnut, crushing Al and Jay to jelly.

Twenty minutes earlier this had seemed like a good idea.

"Steady!"

"Shit!" The unwanted curse cuts at Jay's raw throat. He is near the bow and reckons the perfect opportunity has already come and gone. He tightens his grip, certain they will have to come around for a second try.

Cockburn's earlier words ring in his ears. "Many think movement at sea is an equation. Meet a wave and your bow rises. The boat decelerates, changing the rate of rise in a recursive loop. The hull rolls and yaws, adding to the complexity. But you canna calculate it, you can only feel it."

Jay feels the mystery unfold.

"Now!" Al shouts. "Right fuckin' NOW!" and lets go of his end of the bundled sail.

The Rose Sayer

Nancy Pepper clutches at the cold steel wheel door-lock.

"Goddamn you, Ben, help me."

She strains to release Mr. King and the crewmen trapped inside. They can't wait any longer.

But Ben defies her, holding his place in the universe.

The wheel will not budge.

She prays, willing the water level beyond the sealed door to drop. It too defies her and another man beyond the glass slumps into unconsciousness. He is kept upright, barely, by his friends. Things could not be worse.

Then something long, sleek, and white bursts into the water-filled compartment.

She jerks back from the window. "What the hell!"

Writhing, the thing flails, and then it stops, taut as a bar across the chaotic room, made rigid by internal pressure. Not natural or supernatural, she sees, this is man-made, and somehow it slows the in-rushing ocean. The pump gains ground and the water level behind the door immediately begins to drop.

"Thank God."

She presses her face against the glass. This new thing has plugged the hole, at least partially, at least temporarily. She hears noise behind her and is forced to step aside as crewmen, another damage control team, shoulder past Ben and take over.

Mr. King and his men are carried away to rest and recover, while in knee-deep water, the new team braces the damaged hull and starts to weld a patch in place. For the *Rose Sayer*, the immediate crisis is over.

Ben Irons shuts down his camera.

Gently, Nancy places a hand on his florid cheek. "You stupid son-of-a-bitch." She takes him sternly by the ear.

"Hey!" Ben cries.

"Send the video." She enunciates each syllable for perfect clarity. "Ben I want you to send the video footage you have now, edited or no. There are plenty of hacks at the network who can do the techie work."

"We're too far south," the big man says.

"No, we're not!" she insists.

"Yes, we are," he says. "The network's satellites are equatorial. They orbit around the earth from east to west, not north to south. My uplink dish won't make contact until we're at least a couple of hundred miles further north. We're too far around the earth's curve. Now keep quiet, I've got a lot to do."

That's when she loses it. She is the reporter. She is in charge and they are going to do what she says. She goes to the bridge to look for Langford, but the rat has deserted. All right then, she'll deal directly with the gold-braid.

"Captain." She takes Collins by the elbow and spins him around to face her. "Turn the ship around. Now."

The *Rose Sayer*'s master frowns down on her.

"We've already come about, Miss. We're headed north. We need to get back to port."

"Oh." She is deflated. "Good."

She looks out the big side windows to find a little sailboat has pulled away from the cruise ship. Three men are on deck. One of them waves. She makes a study of ignoring him. Probably a fan.

The Lincoln

Like supplicants praying for a miracle, Clint Rymill and Hank Skelton hunch over the captain's bridge station.

Outside of a military crisis a *SSIXS* call is highly irregular, almost unheard of.

They had to consult the manual on how to use the Submarine Satellite Information Exchange System. The technology is ultra secret and worth more than two boomers, crews included. Both men know they have risked being cashiered if Command doesn't agree that the call is vital.

The uplink panel glows green, connection positive and secure. But the voice that greets them is unexpected.

"Hello, Captain. This here's the president's special advisor, Norman Butchart. Do you know who I am?"

161

"Yes, sir."

"Good. Your admiral is indisposed. But the president directed me to secure his office in the meantime. Please go ahead with your report. Captain Rymill, is it?"

"Yes, sir." Rymill shoots a puzzled look at Skelton. "This will take a bit of explanation. My XO, Mr. Skelton, is here."

"What is this about?"

"Mr. Skelton will upload some data to your screen to illustrate. You have your screen on, Mr. Butchart?"

"Let me see. I'm at the admiral's old desk, yep. Thank you, Shirley. Now you just put on some coffee, honey. Okay boys, I'm all yours."

The Facts

Saturday morning.

A wedding party spills out of the cathedral, into the side garden and under the Whalebone Arch.

A local monument made from the jawbones of a pair of slaughtered blue whales, the Arch forms a kind of hollow, curved pyramid, to honour the glory days of whaling. By local custom, newlyweds have their photos taken standing inside the arch, for luck. Not your average wedding day photo-op, but then Stanley is not your average town.

East of Tierra del Fuego, off the southern tip of South America, lies an archipelago of seven hundred small islands. The Argentines call them the *Islas Malvinas*. To the rest of the world they are the Falklands.

The two main islands (christened West Falkland and East Falkland, with the usual British flair for the obvious) are most famous as the 1982 battleground between Margaret Thatcher's Britain and President/General Leopoldo Galtieri's Argentina, during the eponymously named Falklands War (undoubtedly called The Malvinas War in Buenos Aires). This place has been a bone of contention between those two countries for over a hundred years.

Resource poor, and with a population of only a few thousand, the islands are of no great value in and of themselves. But in the world of two hundred mile resource limits and undersea oil fields, Britain is reluctant to relinquish this crumb of Empire. Besides, the local people are so unrelentingly English it would be like selling off your eccentric grandfather.

These islands are a place of pure wilderness beauty. The beaches teem with penguins and seabirds, seals and sea lions. Powerful Antarctic currents keep its waters abundantly stocked. A few lucky tourists visit these enchanting islands each year, but fishing is the islanders' main source of income.

On the east coast of East Falkland Island, the capital and only town, Stanley, stands on the north shore of a promontory which stretches a long thin finger still farther east out into the Atlantic.

PART FIVE

The Lincoln

"Wake up, Doctor Palmer."

The hand on Graham's shoulder is insistent. Chief Mafri shakes him again.

"The captain and the XO want to see you and the others, ASAP. Grab your socks and drop your . . . "

Eric and Kate join him and they follow Mafri down the corridor. All are sleep-rumpled. Eric yawns and makes a rude whale noise.

"Sorry about that, Chief," he says.

"The captain and XO are talking to the Pentagon," Mafri explains over his shoulder. "A big wig wants to chat with Ring and we need your help."

Graham chews his sleep-gummed lips. "I don't know. That might not be such a wonderful idea." He speaks as Mafri opens the door and motions them in.

"You let me be the judge of that, Mr. Palmer." An unfamiliar voice issues from the speakers, sweet as treacle. "It's Palmer, right?"

"Yes."

"My name is Butchart. I speak for the president. We've digested the XO's executive summary. I have to say, my opinion of navy-types is at an all-time low."

Introductions are made and Butchart continues.

"My bullshit detector is mighty sensitive and right now the needle is off the chart. Fire up your gizmo. I'll do the talking. *Capiche?*"

Graham is reluctant, but Rymill and Skelton already have the system up and running. Kate and Eric mutter assent and take their places. Mafri stands nearby, ready to help.

"Is that the pretty lil scientist that everybody's looking for there? Ms. Sexsmith?" Butchart's accent is thick with anger.

"Present," Kate acknowledges.

"I guess y'all are the cause of this commotion, aren't you, honey? You and your glaciers. And now your boyfriend has a pet whale that can talk. Well ain't that cute."

Kate's face reddens but she holds her tongue. Rymill looks apologetic but says nothing.

"Tell your fish I want to talk to him," Butchart instructs. "Mind that I've got the uplink and I'll be watching both sides of your little picture show here."

Graham patches up a simple call sequence and puts it on a ten second repeat.

After the second call Ring's eloquent reply is heard and a beautiful sequence of images appears on the screen.

Kate automatically starts the interpretation. "A nautilus squid becomes a human in a ship. That's us."

Rymill nods his understanding.

"An adult blue lifts a newborn calf — oh, I'm sure that's an expression of affection. Much nicer than a smiley face, don't you think?"

Kate's pride for Ring seems to have pushed aside any reaction to Butchart's slimy self-satisfaction.

"A blue whale swallows a school of krill."

Eric chuckles. "I'll bet that's *Have you had breakfast?*"

Everyone laughs.

"Can the comedy, people." Butchart's voice is cold, but Graham thinks the president's man may be starting to believe. "We're going to cut to the chase here. I speak, you translate. Got it? Good.

"Here it is. You tell . . . Ring, is it? You tell Ring that his sonar maps are bad things. Very, very bad. That if he or any of his friends show their maps to anyone else, well . . . What would be a suitable stick? I'm not really a carrot guy." Butchart's laugh is dry and mean.

Reluctantly the trio puts the Washington man's words into a coherent train of thought, though they leave out any threat. The song sounds ugly and flat. The scientists understand the paranoid military context, but it's clear from Ring's reply that he is confused.

"Here, try this," Hank Skelton interjects. "Bring up the first map and zoom in on the grid I've marked as A-10. Keep zooming. See — show Ring the problem." He turns to Graham, Kate and Eric. "Ring's map shows the *Lincoln*. No one is supposed to be able to see a boomer. So if the Chinese or anyone else learns how to talk to a blue whale . . . Well, we're sunk. Literally."

"Thank you so much, Mr. Skelton." Butchart's tone is tight. "Y'all tell the whale that. And you tell him that I mean business."

Graham exchanges a look with Eric and Kate.

"Truth," Eric says.

Kate nods. Truth it is. The song they compose is long and melancholy. The images start with Hank Skelton's zoom in on the *Lincoln*'s sound-shadow, followed by a complex theme; the *Lincoln*'s human pod, its nation, is lead by a human/killer whale who will rain harpoons down on blues in a final great slaughter if Ring and his people show anyone else their sonar maps.

The song dives and rises, it resonates off the sub's steel walls until even the three navy men have to wipe their eyes. Hank Skelton mutters something about dust filters.

"Very pretty." Butchart is impatient. "Captain, keep these foreigners under observation. Secure all equipment, computers, software, and notes related to this nonsense. This is a matter of national security and we are not going to have anyone flapping their yaps about talking whales. Is that clear?"

"Sir — "

Rymill is interrupted by a thunderous trumpeting coming from the speakers.

Graham translates, feeling his heart in tune with his new friend.

"Ring says he didn't run from the Fragment and he didn't run from a killer whale pack — and he's not afraid of you, Mr. Butchart."

Eric lets out his rude whale noise and Kate wipes her eyes and picks up the translation.

"Ring says if the human/killer whale — that's you, Mr. Butchart — if you don't get the other nations to *stop* the whale hunt, he *will* tell them where your subs are. All of them. And if they don't understand, he'll show them."

A much longer, louder version of Eric's rude whale noise erupts from the loud speaker.

"That's tellin' him, Ring!" Eric shouts.

"Captain! Shut that damn thing off! Shut it off now!" Butchart is furious. "I want those people in the brig. And I want you to kill that whale immediately. You hear me? Torpedo the son-of-a-bitch!"

"Won't work." Captain Rymill is matter-of-fact. "Our torpedo sensors would never detect a whale." With a mischievous twist to his lips, he adds, "You're not going to suggest we nuke the whales, are you?"

Mafri and the XO look pained by their captain's unaccustomed attempt at humour.

"You've got guns of some kind on that tub, and don't you tell me you don't. You get your men to the surface and you shoot that scum-sucker when it comes up for air and you do it NOW!"

Hank Skelton addresses the captain. "Chain of command, sir."

"My XO is right, Mr. Butchart. You may be the president's special advisor, but you're not in the chain of command. I can't obey your requests to take military action. It would be unconstitutional . . . sir."

"I'll chain-of-command you, you son-of-a-bitch!" Butchart screams. "Hart's going to fry and you're going to fry with him! You maintain this phone line. I'll get you a command — from the commander-in-chief himself!"

They hear Butchart shriek at some poor woman named Shirley to get him the White House, right fuckin' NOW!

Rymill mutes his mike, drags a hand across his mouth, and looks at Skelton and Mafri. "He means it. Hank, I said that I would put these people off my boat when I deemed it safe to do so. I deem it so as of right now. Understand?"

"Sir."

"Mafri," Rymill turns to the chief, "we've got to get these three and their equipment off the *Lincoln*. I need you to find out if any surface vessels are nearby."

Mafri steps away to an intercom handset and speaks urgently to the on-duty sonarman.

"Hank," the captain continues, "we won't surface. They've got to go out the escape trunk."

Skelton blanches. "Jesus, Captain. That's the Antarctic Ocean out there. Even with a raft and survival suits they'll have an hour, tops. Mafri better find someone close to pick them up. I'm not arguing, just laying out parameters."

"I'll run interference." Rymill heads for the door. "I'll take the president's call on the bridge."

Skelton quickly puts out the order and a group of crewmen arrives on the run. Two are sent to ready the escape trunk and the rest to collect the watertight containers needed for the equipment.

"We'll send your equipment out the escape hatch first," the commander explains, "in containers, roped to a life raft."

"Just a minute, Mr. Skelton," Kate breaks through the clamour. "Graham, we ought to tell Ring. So he knows why we're not talking."

"Tell Ring what?" asks the XO.

"At least let him know that Nautilus is on his side," says Graham.

"We should warn him to get the hell out of here and keep quiet for a few days," Eric suggests.

"Okay. Hurry up." Skelton waves them on and the crewmen stand ready to dismantle the system the moment they're finished.

Kate, Graham, and Eric compose the message, trading elegance for brevity. Then the plugs are pulled.

"What Ring might do," Graham says, "is anyone's guess."

≪≪≪

Minutes later they are inside the sub's escape chamber.

"Wait. Wait." Kate is being zipped into a bizarre outfit. "This isn't right. It's made for a man. It's tight in all the wrong places."

"We're trained professionals, ma'am," the navy frogman assures her. "I've got you covered." He produces a pointed hood that resembles a high-temperature firefighter's headpiece.

"There's no mask?" The edge in Kate's voice sharpens. "Where's the mouth piece? How am I supposed to breathe?"

"It's okay, ma'am. They're full body dry-suits. They're supposed to look like this."

He secures the hood over her head and then fits Eric and Graham.

"This is a mistake." Kate is insistent. "This is a practice suit."

"It's okay. It's okay." The frogman tightens a strap. "You just need to calm down." Then he clips a length of nylon cord to her belt. "You're linked to Dr. Lawson and Dr. Palmer, to keep you from getting separated."

He vanishes through the bulkhead door. Only the spinning wheel that locks them inside shows that anyone exists outside this tiny chamber.

Graham is worried. Something is going on with Kate. He keeps his eyes on her.

"Katie, are you okay?" Eric's voice is muffled.

"Claustrophobia. You probably both think I'll crack." She gives a clumsy thumbs-up inside the dry-suit mittens.

With the door closed the room is small. They are squeezed by the crushing pressures beyond the steel walls.

In a few moments the valves open and water rushes in, swirls around their calves, rising swiftly, past their hips, necks, over the crinkling plastic face plates to fill the tiny chamber.

Surfacing

A bubble of precious air is trapped inside her hood and Kate gulps at it, unable to stop. Her breath fogs the suddenly chilled plastic. She rises, floating, trapped against the steel plate ceiling.

They said the ceiling would open! She pushes but has no leverage. It won't budge.

"Something's gone wrong, something's wrong!"

But there's no one to hear her.

A muffled clang splits the ceiling wide and she is thrust into darkness. Sudden cold and pressure jolt her. The water is as black as ink. A tiny flashlight bulb glows inside her hood. Without that, the abysmal darkness would be complete and she feels she would go mad.

Water rushes past her as the buoyant suit speeds her toward the surface. The faceplate ripples with the flow, like it might shred at any moment. Her breath is acrid in her own nostrils, as bitter as a horse's blow. Seconds creep away into a darkness where anything might lurk.

"Please God, let it be over."

She can't see the other two; only feel the drag of the cord that connects them, clipped to her belt. Lighter than the men, she must be rising faster. A predatory fear catches that thought and leaps to its own conclusion — *I'm not rising. They're dragging me down!*

She gropes for the clip. The damned mittens refuse her purchase.

She tries to bite the fingertips, to pull the clumsy things off with her teeth and succeeds in ramming the plastic plate into her nose. It holds and in the next moment she bobs, a cork on the surface at last. The tug of the cord slackens. Eric and

Graham's suits appear. Strobe lights on their hoods begin to flash.

It's strange to be in the world again. Cold fingers its way in, penetrating the suit. The air, now snorkeled into the hood, is briny and rich, and her little window frames a surreal seascape. It teems with pristine white shapes, icebergs, like up-thrust rocks in a raked Japanese garden.

Behind the bergs, the horizon is also white and pitches oddly upward, out of sync with the expected line of sea and sky. Her brain makes the shift and she sees it.

The Fragment has created its own horizon, shrinking the icebergs to pond toys. She and the men might be two miles away or a half-dozen. Nothing in her field of vision gives any sense of scale. The belt clip tugs again. It turns her and she sees the slab side of a sloop a few yards away. Graham is clambering up a ladder, and men in cold-weather gear are reaching down to help him.

Eric floats nearby, head and shoulders above the water line. The name on the stern of the boat proclaims someone's admiration for a woman named *Marcy*. The cord pulls her closer and then a strangely familiar face hovers over the gunwale — a face last seen on a computer screen in her Scott Base lab, back a dozen lifetimes ago.

"Jay Traljesic?"

Traljesic disappears as a fountain of water rains over the sloop and Kate hears Graham's shout and the boatmen's cries of alarm.

She knows what it must be. Ring is spouting!

He passes under the *Marcy*'s keel and glides under Kate, gently bumping her boots. Then, rising, he lifts her out of the ocean.

She stands up on his back, Venus on the half shell, water streaming away, and feels a familiar rumble through the soles of her feet. She pulls her head free of the hood and shouts to the men.

"Nautilus!" she cries. "He said Nautilus!"

The Marcy

"Jay," Al declares, "that makes the whole trip worth it. The cold. The damp. Everything. The whale and the girl. Just to see your face."

Blair Cockburn slaps the younger newsman on the back. "Best shut your mouth. You'll drown if it rains."

By the time the men recovered their wits, Ring had held Kate up long enough for her to stroll directly onto the *Marcy*, like a princess taking the airs.

Kalhua-laced teas are distributed to all hands. Explanations are made and exclaimed at.

When doubts are expressed, Graham hooks a thumb over his shoulder.

"Did you see the thirty metres of evidence that's swimming outside the boat?"

"The past quarter hour," Blair Cockburn concedes, "has made me a bit more credulous than normal. First, a couple of dozen plastic bottles pop to the surface with flashing lights attached. We snagged one and read a message from someone named Commander Skelton, asking us to signal receipt by starting and stopping our engine three times in quick succession. Which we did. And to stand by to rescue three castaways. Then a life raft and some cargo pods appeared — "

"Are they safe?" asks Graham.

"Aye, they're safe."

The equipment pods are opened and despite the tight quarters the scientists make short work of reconstituting an abbreviated version of the sub's whale lab. The *Lincoln*'s crewmen have included the yellow hydrophone transmitter/receiver, which now dangles overboard, trailing the *Marcy*'s stern. Once all is in place, communication is re-established with the big blue whale, while Al and Jay film and interview the scientists.

Later, they all convene on deck.

"It's time for me to go home to Scotland," Cockburn mutters, looking out at the whale and the Fragment, "because now I've seen everything."

"I'd say you're right, Mr. Cockburn," Eric concurs. "We should all go to Scotland. Or at least somewhere far from here, and take Ring with us."

"Time for a war council." The Scotsman's hand is on the tiller. "If you're done your television work, we need to decide what to do next."

"Eric is right," Graham agrees. "We should get out. The US authorities want Ring dead and us in custody." He looks at Al, Jay, and Cockburn. "I'm sorry, but that probably includes you, too, now that you have seen everything."

"Bloody English!" Cockburn growls.

"No, Mr. Cockburn," Kate corrects him. "They're Americans."

"To me, Miss," he says, "they're all bloody English."

Eric nods his general agreement. "The *Lincoln* might not come after us. But this is the US government. They can have another warship out here in days."

"Or jets here in hours," Jay adds his own grim assessment.

The cabin is quiet.

Al finally speaks up. "I've got an idea." He looks at the Scotsman. "But you aren't going to like it."

The Lincoln

Clint Rymill stands at the centre of the *Lincoln's* bridge cradling a hand-held mike.

Though it's not according to regulations, he's had the *SSIXIS* voice line patched into the boat-wide PA system. If he's going ahead with this he may need plenty of witnesses.

It's Lieutenant Prudholm's watch and Rymill tells his Second Officer to monitor the boat. He will have his hands full with other matters.

A minute later Hank Skelton steps in and gives him two big thumbs up. Their passengers are on their way. Good luck and Godspeed.

It doesn't take long to patch through the conference call. Butchart has already brought the POTUS in. The man clearly has pull.

"Mr. President," Butchart's voice is smooth, "this is the officer I tol' you about."

"Captain Rymill, this is the president speaking." The tone is calm and reassuring, like a preacher who knows he has the ear of God. "My good friend, Mr. Butchart, has briefed me on your little misunderstanding. Now, this here is an order from your commander-in-chief. Arrest your three prisoners and kill that whale, just like Norman asked you to. Understood, son?"

Rymill feels eight years old. "I'm sorry, sir. I am unable to comply. The people you are referring to, the former passengers, are no longer aboard the *Lincoln*."

"What are you talking about, Captain?"

"And, respectfully, sir, I decline the order to kill the whale, sir."

The president is composed. "Why is that, Captain?"

"Sir, the Uniform Code of Military Justice requires all military personnel to refuse an order that is unlawful, sir." Rymill presses his fingernails into the page, underscoring the relevant line in the Code that lies open in front of him.

"I fail to understand. How can it be an unlawful order to be told to kill a whale, Captain?"

"Because, sir, the whale, his name is Ring, is a non-combatant. A citizen of a foreign nation . . . which we are not at war with . . . sir."

There it was, ending with a preposition that Winston Churchill would've been proud of. It sounded much better before he had to say it out loud.

"This . . . *is* a whale we're talking about, isn't it, Norman?"

"Yes, sir."

"Okay. Captain. Let's just say that I've declared war on this one particular whale, shall we?"

"Sorry, sir. You can't. The president can't declare war. Only Congress can declare war, sir."

The silence is ominous. The pressure outside the hull is nothing to what Rymill feels in here.

Butchart cuts in. "It's a clear and present danger to the security of the U S of A, Mr. President. You can issue a National Security Directive, sir."

"Norman, you've written most of those for me in the past. Why don't you scribble one out and I'll sign it right now. Will that do it for you, Captain?"

He has offered Rymill one final out.

Bridge crewmen exchange worried looks and the boat seems to hold its breath.

Rymill comes to attention and salutes. "No. Thank you, sir." He flips a page of the Military Justice book and extracts a sheet of paper. "I'm handing my resignation to my executive officer, Mr. Skelton. You know what they used to say, sir, suppose they gave a war and nobody came?"

He hands the paper and microphone to Skelton. The XO reluctantly takes them. The dry mouth sounds that issue from the speaker tell a tale of executive branch fury.

Finally the president speaks again. "All right then. Acting-Captain Skelton — put this man under arrest for treason and carry out — "

"No, sir." Skelton pops off his commander's bars and drops them with the microphone on the table.

"Who the hell's in charge down there!" screams Butchart.

"I've got it, Mr. President. Lieutenant Prudholm reporting, sir. Taking command. Make me aware of your instructions, sir, and the *Lincoln* will comply. You can count on it."

"Good man, Prudholm. See to that whale. And make sure you get those people back. Use whatever means necessary."

"Yes, sir. I can advise that prior to your call Commander Skelton was in contact with a civilian sloop on the surface, requesting they take on the three scientists — "

From the sonar station comes a loud CLICK!

Lieutenant Prudholm and the rest turn.

"I'm sorry, .sir, but SSIXS is offline," Mafri announces. "And so is sonar." One by one he flicks panel switches until the whole sonar board is black.

Before the word "mutiny" can claw its ugly way up Prudholm's throat, the air is filled with clicks as a room full of men, men who have become Ring's friends, stand up, shut down and step away from their stations.

The USS *Lincoln* will not make war on the whales today.

Standard operating procedure would've put a wingman in the air off his six, but the pilot of the naval strike jet — designated "one-niner" — is on a long-range and decidedly solo mission.

Whatever is up, he's quite certain the mission parameters put him inside a CIA or NSA op. It's a real "need-to-know," "keep the operator in the dark" mushroom fest.

He's been given a waypoint, 64 degrees south, 87 degrees west, not an actual destination. On the map it's as blank a bit of ocean as far from anything worth fighting for as he can imagine. No target info either. And the weapons load-out was both strange and specific. Twin gun-pods and no missiles. That last bit leaves him feeling pretty naked. Nobody flies without air-to-air missiles any more.

It's time to break radio silence.

"Control, I'm at Angels plus twenty-nine thousand. On target location in under two minutes. Hey, Control. I spy one mother of an ice flow down there. Copy?"

"Roger, one-niner, cut the chatter and bring it down to Angels plus one thousand. I say again, Angels plus one thousand feet altitude for your strike pass. Over."

"Copy that, Control. Descending to Angels plus one thousand. Arming weapons now. I say again, the pickle switch is on. Over."

"Roger, one-niner. You're looking for a suspected Al-Qaeda vessel. Wait for my green-go before live fire. Do you copy?"

"Copy that, Control. I have a visual. Looks like a cruise ship. Five hundred footer. Is that my target? Copy?"

"Copy, one-niner. Wait one." A dummy light shows Control gone to *Mute* then returns to *On*. "Negative. I say again. Negative on the cruise ship. That is not your target. You're looking for a small sailing sloop. Over."

"Roger, Control. Looking for a small sailboat. Say, Control, is the sloop out to attack the cruise ship? Over."

"Cut the chatter, one-niner. Eyes up. Over."

"Roger, Control. Eyes up. With so many bergs, radar can't pick anything out of the clutter. Lots of fog. Hard to tell. Wait one. Something . . . Control, I have a visual on the sloop."

"Report one-niner."

"Our bad boy's moored tight to an iceberg, trying to lie doggo. Over."

"Roger, one-niner. Wait one. We have green for the strike. I say again. You are go on the strike. The Director says don't spare the ammo, sonny. Over."

"Roger, Control. Rolling for pass."

"Keep your cool, son."

"Cool here, Control."

Strike jet one-niner has enough ammo for five seconds of continuous fire. Not bullets in the usual sense, these. The size of pop bottles, heavy with a spent uranium core, tough with a tungsten jacket, they are meant to pierce tanks, not a trim little sailboat.

It only takes three seconds to march a chainsaw of bullets down the iceberg's side and into the boat's hull. In and out, they hole her port and starboard, each wound doubled.

"Control, one-niner. We have a positive splash. Target terminated. No secondary explosions, Control. Wasn't it supposed be armed? Over."

This time a new voice responds, as familiar in cadence as one-niner's hometown Sunday-school teacher.

"This is the president. Cut the chatter, son. You got that? Over?"

"This is one-niner. Yes, sir. I copy. Zipping my lip, sir. Over."

"Say," a new, third voice joins in, "y'all don't see a lil' old whale down there, do you son?"

"Say again, sir? Did you say a whale, sir? Over."

"A whale, yes, that's right. A whale."

"Uh, no, sir. I don't."

"No spray from a blowhole?"

"No, sir."

Control comes back on the line. "Roger, one-niner. The boss said good job, head on home. Over and out."

The Rose Sayer

It's a chancy thing, to moor a boat to an iceberg. In the latter part of World War II, when advances in radar made life difficult for the German wolf-packs, desperate U-boat captains tried it in the North Atlantic, with mixed success. If the berg rolls you won't even slow it down. You're just a bug on the windshield. But if you're trying to hide from an air search, it's a risk you might be willing to take. For the *Marcy* that gamble fails. The *Mark I* eyeball finds her.

From the promenade deck of the *Rose Sayer* hundreds of passengers watch the strike jet roar up into the sky. A victory roll carves wingtip streamers out of the chilled air.

"Hoo-wee! Did you see that honey? Woosh, wham-o!" Sam Garry, the Florida carpet king, is pumped. "First, rocking it up close with that iceberg, now this. I'm gonna give the captain a tip for sure. Best cruise ever!"

Garry turns to another couple. "Remember, I told you at dinner the first night on board, about why I booked a White

Star cruise? We saw that report, right honey, where their ship was on the front lines, right in the middle of a Navy exercise."

The Floridian throws a sloppy salute skyward. "God bless America and our men in uniform."

The show is over and most of the onlookers disperse, to go back inside for hot toddies and snacks, and to chatter nervously about what they've witnessed, and wonder what's next.

Other groups have other theories about the sinking of the little vessel. James Bond-style high intrigue is a favoured theme, while a war-on-drugs smuggling angle has its own advocates. Some link the air strike to the Fragment, but no one is even close to what is really going on.

Three hardier souls remain on deck, hidden in their parkas, to say farewell to a lost friend.

"She was a beauty." Loss thickens Cockburn's accent.

"Will there be a *Marcy V*?" Jay asks the Scotsman. His throat is still tender, but seems to be on the mend.

"Aye, Jay. Some say I'm stubborn." Cockburn pulls back the hood of his coat. "Think I'll have another word with Captain Collins."

Jay watches him climb the stairs to the bridge deck.

Al Milliken peers over the side rail. "So long as Ring stays near the *Rose Sayer* he'll be okay."

Jay joins him in time to catch a glimpse of disappearing flukes. "Come on. You promised Xena Princess-Reporter an interview up top."

On the helicopter pad they find big Ben Irons balancing his steady-cam like an artist's paintbrush.

"I remember the good old days," says Al. "CNN is lucky to have that guy. I'll introduce you to him later."

Nancy Pepper — "Xena Princess-Reporter" — is radiant.

Jay is envious for a moment. This story is going to make her career. And the footage Ben would've caught of the strike jet shooting up the little boat would be the topper. Next stop, network anchor!

Nancy shares centre stage with Kate, their contrasting hair and skin tones a cameraman's dream. And then Kate and Graham explain what it all means, while Eric provides colour commentary.

Nancy waves Jay and Al into the picture and they all watch the vapour trails of an old world they both hope and fear will soon fade away.

Wake

Blair Cockburn is pleased that, for tonight at least, Captain Collins has closed off one of the *Rose Sayer*'s small bars, turning it into a private lounge for the *Marcy*'s six castaways.

The room is a welcome haven from the day's chaos. A fine spread of food has been laid out, drinks are "on the house" and the bar staff has been sent elsewhere.

"I can only stay for a short time." Collins calls for the group's attention. "Captain Cockburn, I can't tell you how much I owe to you, your vessel, and your crew, for your assistance earlier today."

Jay smiles and winks at Blair. "Crew, he said. We're crew."

"Aye, Jay, you'll do." The Scotsman turns back to Collins. "Nothing one sailor wouldn't do for another. And we have you to thank for saving our hides in return. Us, and our three jetsam passengers too."

"There must be a word for double castaways." Eric shakes his head. "Rescued twice in one day."

"We're grateful to all of you," Kate says.

"And for helping Ring," Graham adds.

"It's the least I could do." Collins turns to Blair. "Captain? The *Marcy IV*. Do you mind if I ask what happened to the other three?"

Cockburn looks at Jay, and the newsman provides the standard one word answer. "Sank."

"And Captain Collins?" Al asks. "I feel like I ought to know who *Rose Sayer* was."

"Ah, that." Collins pauses. "The grandfather of our current chairman had a crush on Katherine Hepburn, so the story goes. Rose Sayer was her character in *The African Queen*. I think it was meant to impress her. In any case, White Star has had a liner by that name ever since."

"She lives up to the name." Al pats the bar's granite top affectionately. "Tough bird."

"You were lucky we were still nearby." Collins turns to Blair. "You've lost a good ship today. She deserves a proper wake."

"Aye," Cockburn agrees, "she does."

Collins produces a bottle of scotch. Seven glasses are christened with a dram of whiskey.

Jay stands. "I'd like to tell you a story, about another ship, if I may."

Cockburn knows it's his permission that the newsman is seeking. "What better place for stories, than a wake?" he says.

"It's about 'ship's luck'." Jay speaks in a low voice, but he's starting to sound like his old self. "A while ago, for the show, I interviewed a Canadian marine archeologist. There had been exciting news about a find in the high Arctic."

"The wreck of the *Erebus*?" Kate asks.

"That's right," says Jay.

"Oh, yes, I remember." Kate explains to the others: "To hear our Prime Minister tell it, you'd think he'd discovered the site all by himself."

"Too many Clive Cussler novels, I suspect," Blair offers. "I've had a few passengers like that."

"After the interview," Jay continues, "the archeologist told Al and me about the one they haven't found yet, the HMS Terror."

Jay gestures at his sore throat, and Al takes a turn at the storytelling.

"The Terror," Al explains, "was a 'bomb ship', built by the British. Not literally a bomb, but a ship designed to carry heavy mortars to fire shells over the walls of fortresses."

"Ordinary cannons," Jay says, "were fired horizontally and spent their recoil by kicking backwards."

"But," Al adds, "because mortars fire close to straight up, a ship that carried them had to be built especially strong to withstand the downward recoil."

"Newton's Third Law," Eric interjects. "To every action there is an equal and opposite reaction."

Jay and Al laugh. "Remind me to show you the Rookland video later," Jay says.

"Anyway," Al returns to the story, "during the War of 1812, Terror was one of the British ships that fired on Fort McHenry at Baltimore."

"*And the rockets' red glare, the bombs bursting in air*." In a rich baritone Captain Collins intones a verse from his national anthem. "Francis Scott Keys was there," he adds.

"So, you're saying Terror inspired 'The Star Spangled Banner'?" Cockburn asks and can't help but think there's a George W. Bush joke in there somewhere.

"Well, helped inspire, yes," Al continues. "*Terror* survived that war and later, when the Royal Navy needed two especially strong ships for James Ross' expedition to explore Antarctica, they naturally chose two bomb ships, the *Erebus* and the *Terror.*"

"We know this part." Kate turns to Eric and Graham. "That's our Ross. The Ross Sea, Ice Shelf, and Island are named after him."

"And," Graham adds, "the two volcanoes on Ross Island, Mount Erebus and Mount Terror, are named after those two ships."

"Those are the smoking mountains from Ring's story about Long-Throat." Eric speaks with reverence. "What strange connections."

"But I'll bet you don't know this part." Jay raises an authoritative finger. "The *Erebus* and the *Terror* sailed north on a new mission — "

"The Franklin expedition," Kate interrupts. "I'm sorry Jay. I know this is your story, but a cousin on my mother's side ran the William Kennedy museum north of Winnipeg. Lady Franklin twice appointed Kennedy to lead searches to find her husband."

Cockburn raps the table in delight. "Mind your open mouth, Jay. Remember? In case of rain?"

"For any who might not know." Al gives Kate a wry smile. "Sir John Franklin took *Erebus* and *Terror* in search of the Northwest Passage."

"There, having travelled to both ends of the earth . . . " Jay's tone suggests that he's come to the point of his story, "luck ran out for the *Erebus* and the *Terror*. Locked in the crushing ice pack, the Franklin expedition was never heard from again." He casts a glance at Cockburn. "It is most fortunate for all of us here, for the *Rose Sayer*, and especially for Mr. King and his men, that luck was generous to the *Marcy* to the very end."

Glasses are raised and as one they speak, "To the *Marcy*."

"Thank you for that story, Jay, Al." Cockburn touches a callused finger to the corner of his eye. "Wakes are a fine place for old stories of ships and the sea. Some ships, like some people, have extraordinary lives." He rises. "Shortly after we set off on this voyage, the lads and I spent some time looking at my Antarctic charts. Precise and detailed they are, the product of four hundred years of British naval guts and blood.

"Captain Pringle Stokes of the Royal Navy, for one, spent month after gale-lashed month at sea off the Horn trying to chart 'the hard' — the islands and reefs that waited to tear his ship to pieces, were he to make a single mistake.

"Alas, poor Pringle. More a man for battles than a surveyor — some say he fought with Nelson at Trafalgar — his fifteen months at the Horn resulted in badly flawed charts.

"Unable to face the humiliation, Pringle took his own life and thus left his ship, the HMS *Beagle*, of which you may've heard, to be reassigned."

"Jesus. No kidding." Jay looks at Al.

"His successor, one Captain Robert FitzRoy, invited a certain English beetle enthusiast to be the *Beagle*'s naturalist.

"It was only after that chance to see the wider world that this man, Charles Darwin by name, came to write his great theory.

"Does it not appeal to your sense of irony," Cockburn adds more Scotch to his glass, "that the future of mankind can pivot on such invisible things as a chart-maker's injured pride?"

He looks into his glass and then at Graham. "And it does my heart good to think that when the story of Dr. Palmer and the first contact with the blue whales is told, that the *Marcy*'s name will live on, as a small part of that story."

The seven glasses are emptied a second time and Cockburn turns to Graham.

"I'd like to be of use to you, Dr. Palmer," he says, "and to your blue friends, too."

"Of course, Captain."

Blair recognizes the Maori scientist's natural caution. Many of New Zealand's earliest colonists were from Scotland.

"Here's what I have in mind." He spreads his hands. "You tell me if any of it makes sense. I'll be meeting with the insurance broker and then picking out a new sloop once we get to harbour, and . . . "

Stanley, Falkland Islands

Dawn. Today the cathedral is empty though the sun still touches both the spire and the Whalebone Arch.

Yesterday's television news reports about the Fragment received some local attention, but icebergs cruise past Stanley every year. A few run aground on the shallows. No one is alarmed.

One more iceberg, even a very large one, won't cause anyone much inconvenience.

But today no one is in church. No one seeks good luck under the Whalebone Arch. Today every resident of Stanley shivers on the low ridge south of town, looking south, out to sea.

That southern horizon is a ribbon of glittering white. As far as the eye can see, the Wall rises up out of the sea, like the White Cliffs of Dover come to call on this farthest flung English possession.

The people of Stanley watch and no one speaks. The air grows colder. Sinuous fog slithers from the tabletop mountain of white, across the narrowing miles. This is no iceberg to be stranded on the beach.

"Someone ought to do something," the mayor says.

No one does. They are birds transfixed by a viper. Amid growing awe and fear, the islanders watch the Fragment's western tip strike bottom south of Stanley with a sound like Thor's hammer, and the ground trembles.

It is a titanic train wreck. The sounds are tremendous. Ice shrieks, hell is unleashed. People fall to the ground, hands on their ears, unable to muffle the sound. The Fragment does not slow. No jerk or momentary stop hints that the leading edge has touched the sea bottom. It keeps coming, rising higher and higher out of the ocean.

Magical sea-carved shapes appear. Atlantean caves vomit seawater. Minarets of ice topple forward and break to grease the Fragment's slipway. The current's speed here is fifteen miles an hour and the Fragment matches that, inch for inch.

Everyone can see the danger. People run for their cars to try and escape up the long peninsula.

Some make it to higher ground inland, ahead of the on-rushing ice. Most do not.

When the Fragment is gone, the promontory where Stanley once stood is polished smooth. No trace of human presence remains. The Fragment leaves behind a few cubic miles of ice, a tiny wound.

It moves north and then east again, headed for Africa.

"Norman, I am not very happy."

"No, Mr. President."

"Your handling of these matters, this Fragment, the foreign scientists and the blue whale has been poor. You have placed both of us under intense scrutiny."

"Yes, sir."

"And the Stanley Disaster is not theoretical. You told me that this Sexsmith woman's ideas were unsubstantiated."

"Yes, sir."

"The media floodgates have opened, Norman. Disturbing comparisons have been made."

"Yes, sir."

"One item in particular caught my attention. Nancy Pepper said your ice shelf was 'Half the size of Kentucky, and it could cover the coast of South Carolina from end to end.' Now, can you imagine how that makes a Southern boy feel?"

"Yes, sir."

"Well, some of our friends in the Senate have suggested that I follow the old Eskimo example and have you put out on this ice flow to die."

"Yes, sir."

"Do you have nothing to say but 'Yes, sir,' Norman?"

"No, sir. I do have some thoughts, if I may."

"Please."

"Well first, we can make good use of David Rookland. You remember him. He was caught up in that business with Admiral Hart's leak."

"Oh, yes."

"Because of that, Rookland has gained some notoriety as a scientist that the military was trying to rush to judgment."

"Go on."

"We have Rookland resurface on the major networks to assure the public that no iceberg has ever passed the equator. I've checked. That is a bona fide fact."

"I like facts that favour our position."

"Then, through back channels only, we encourage the European Union to convene a conference of the world's leading climate scientists to discuss the situation and offer their solutions."

"Good, Norman. No politician has ever gone wrong delaying a decision for the results of an egghead study."

"Yes, sir. And later, if you have to dismiss a European-made solution, well, that always plays well to the party's base."

"Did we kill that whale?"

"Who can criticize a president for trying to protect America's atomic submarine fleet from an animal?"

"Not what I asked, Norman."

"Those sonar maps seriously destabilize our international relations, with friend and foe alike."

"Why are you hedging, Norman?"

"Well, no. We didn't kill the whale."

"For heaven's sake, Norman, where's the upside to all this?"

"You're forced to recall the missile-sub fleet to port, Mr. President."

"That's an upside?"

"Yes, sir. To protect the lives of our brave servicemen. Stay with me. Why put them needlessly in harm's way? Call on other nations to do the same, demonstrating your leadership as a man of peace."

"Sounds risky."

"For such statesmanship a Nobel Prize might seem appropriate, sir."

"Would you say so, Norman?"

"Why not? Then announce a four percent force reduction in the navy. That should cover the missile-sub crews, sub-tender personnel, dry-dock and port facility people, and so on, that we can let go."

"Many of those ports are in districts that have elected my opponents."

"The job losses can be laid at the door of whale-lovers, sir."

"That will refocus quite a lot of anger, Norman."

"And I've saved the best for last, sir. By docking just these fourteen subs you can cut the Navy's operating costs by about one-third! Nearly fifty billion dollars."

"A third? My, my. That's excluding the Marines, I hope? I do like the Marines."

"Yes, sir. The Marines keep their forty billion."

"Good. 'Send in the Marines' sounds so much more presidential than 'Send in the Navy.'"

"Quite so, Mr. President. With that kind of money available for reallocation, our friends in the Senate can be made to see the error of their ways."

"As I've often said, every crisis has a lining of silver."

Copenhagen, Denmark

"The committee recognizes independent delegate, Doctor K. Sexsmith ."

It is ten days after the Stanley disaster, and the hastily convened European Fragment Conference is already in session.

The chairman is a distinguished elder German scientist who sounds to Kate like Henry Kissinger. He is flanked by experts from four other European countries. Kate recognizes the committee's heavy hitter, a French glaciologist, Professor Arceneau of the CNRS at Grenoble, seated on the chairman's right.

"Thank you, Mr. Chairman."

Her presence here has drawn the media out in force. A dozen extra microphones are clipped to her podium and twice as many TV cameras share Kate's space. Half are focused on her. The others scan and record the panel. She sees ties and jackets adjusted and hair carefully smoothed back.

Jay has helped her prep for this, so rather than launch into her presentation she waits to see which panel member will feel compelled to make opening remarks.

"*Excusez-moi*," the Frenchman begins, "for the record, we must acknowledge that the American government has laid charges of espionage, theft of government property, and escape from lawful custody against you and your colleagues, Dr. Lawson and Dr. Palmer."

"Yes." Kate is pleased that her voice is firm. "But we will be exonerated."

"I certainly hope you're right."

"Thank you for your good wishes, *monsieur*." She ignores the slight and gives the reporters their first soundbite. "Gentlemen, the Fragment will kill more than twenty thousand people before the end of this year."

"One moment." The chairman's face is stern. "It is unique, but now that we're aware of its existence, the berg will pose little threat to life." He turns and gives the floor to the Frenchman.

"My students have been working furiously on a computer model." The glaciologist speaks with an easy confidence. "It shows the main body will break up before it reaches the tropics. The pieces will disperse, circle the South Atlantic, and melt away. The model — "

"Excuse me," Kate leans into the microphones, "but your students' model is based on high altitude glaciers, not sea-borne ice, and not on this scale. Your students have missed important variables and, as they say, several 'spherical cows' lurk inside their calculations."

"Doctor, please," the chairman sits forward, "you needn't be confrontational. We're all friends here. One never has perfect data — "

"And your heat transference figures are way off base. Alpine glaciers shed their cold melt water quickly because it runs downhill. That can't happen with the Fragment. I'm sorry to be blunt but that's garbage-in, garbage out."

"Dr. Sexsmith," the chairman smiles gently, "I know you've only recently returned from Antarctic waters, but even you cannot deny the warmth of the equatorial ocean. The temperature gradient is substantial."

"Yes," Kate holds the man's gaze, "but those are surface temperatures. And the professor's model fails to take into account that the Fragment has created its own guarding moat of cold, pure water."

"Won't the cold water simply sink away?"

The German's question is one Kate's been expecting. "No. Cold *fresh* water is less dense than warm *salt* water. It won't fall away. It will float, and stay with the Fragment."

The chairman seems genuinely interested. "Please go on."

"Sir, we know the fresh water of a great river like the Amazon remains unmixed with the ocean's salt water for many miles beyond the shoreline. Following the same principles, the Fragment has created its own heat shield, like a skirt of icewater."

"Elegantly put, *Professeur* Sexsmith. That is something we will investigate," Professor Arceneau says, "but even if it is true, the tropical sun will blast the ice with a thousand watts per square metre."

"Oh, it will melt," Kate focuses her attention on the other men on the panel, "given time. But the ice shelf's surface is pure white. That reflective Albedo will cut the thousand watts by four-fifths, to two hundred. Then add the dense white cloud that will condense out of the humid air to cover the Fragment."

Kate sees one of the committee's lesser members is making notes and doing his own quick calculations. The man speaks up, "The cloud cuts the sun again, so only one-fifth *of* one-fifth will get through."

"Correct." Kate silently thanks Eric for the next comparison. "The thousand watts drops to two hundred, and then to only forty watts. We all know how weak a forty-watt light bulb is. I wouldn't pit one against this seven-hundred-metre-thick monster."

"So. Good." The German nods like a kindly grandfather, left and right to the committee. "We have found common ground at last, Doctor. With time it will melt. We've also heard from witnesses who urge that we remain optimistic. That we explore ways to make use of all that fresh water, to make it available for the good of all. We could look on it as an unexpected resource."

Kate has heard this before. "Sir, don't let yourself be sidetracked. The resilience and destructive power of this thing must be our main concern."

"You're certainly confident in your views, Doctor." The chairman sits back. "Let us say, for the sake of argument, that you are right, yes? We've learned the lesson of Stanley. Evacuation inland from the coastline of those threatened, just as is done for hurricanes, will prevent significant loss of life."

"I'm sorry, but earlier Professor Arceneau said the Fragment would break up and remain in the South Atlantic. But it's still bigger than Switzerland. The whole country, gentlemen. There's a high probability that it will cross the equator. Once that happens there's a real chance the Gulf Stream will carry it northeast. It could drive straight up the English Channel. Professor, at its narrowest, how wide is the Channel?"

The Frenchman pauses. "At Calais and Dover it narrows to about thirty kilometres." He turns to the cameras. "For our American friends, that's twenty miles."

"The Fragment is a hundred miles wide, two hundred miles long," Kate continues, "so say goodbye to every English seaport from Plymouth to Dover and every French coastal city from Brest to Calais. That's easily five million people displaced. Countless billions of dollars of damage, plus the disruption of the fifth and sixth largest economies on the planet."

"Please, Doctor." The chairman taps his fountain pen on the table. "Such examples are imaginative, but we must not inflame the passions of the public."

The chairman starts to say more but the French delegate gestures for forbearance. "*Professeur* Sexsmith, we must not make the public think you are the Greeks' cursed Cassandra. Rest assured, we will hear your prophecies, and weigh them justly. Please, *continue.*"

"*Merci.*" Kate wonders if the man is finally listening. "Past the Dover Narrows, what would it do to Belgium and the Netherlands? The Hague, Amsterdam, gone like Stanley? The Dutch dikes will fold like balsawood. For those countries the devastation would surpass the worst of World War Two, compressed into just a few days. With that shoreline shredded, a worldwide depression would be the least of our problems."

"In that highly unlikely event," the chairman says, "I'm sure that Germany and the whole European Union would stand by our friends and allies, and, well, yes, local preparations should be made, of course, and evacuation assistance provided, where and when needed. But that's certainly nothing beyond the world community's capacity to deal with."

"Respectfully, Mr. Chairman, the world has faced plenty of hurricanes, tidal waves, and earthquakes. But we have no historical event to compare with the Fragment. And Europe isn't the only place in danger. There are millions of people at risk on the Caribbean islands. Many are poorly educated and have no resources of their own. When do we move them? How do we move them? Who is prepared to take them in? And based on Stanley, who is prepared to take them in on a permanent basis?"

"We are not blind to these concerns, Doctor. But we must take a balanced view. We cannot simply adopt an alarmist approach. Our scientific community's reputation for sound council is too important to risk. I do hope you'll continue to work with us. Your input is truly valued."

"Of course, Mr. Chairman."

As she feared it would, ultimately the committee's report boils down to "hope for the best."

Tropic Passage

For a time, with Jay and Al in her corner, the I-TV network is willing to give Kate a bully pulpit.

"But," Jay tells her, "for the American public, no matter how impressive our film footage, the Fragment is a problem that belongs to others, like land mines or imperialist guilt."

"And it's just too slow," Al adds, "slowly crossing the South Atlantic, and then a slow spin up the West Coast of Africa — it's stretching into weeks. It's too long in the news cycle."

"You can see my projections are correct." Kate hands them her latest graphs. "The interaction of extreme cold with high tropical humidity has created a cloud that shields the ice from the sun."

Jay agrees. "And the pictures from space of that anvil cloud are spectacular."

"But soon," Al concludes, "it will be 'Seen one, seen them all.'"

The Fragment

A variety of nations regularly dispatch airplanes to probe the cloud with radar. The rate of change is not encouraging. Curving west under the bulge of Africa, the juggernaut could devastate the coastlines of any of the countries it passes by. Estimates vary, but even though the Fragment has been on the move for over a hundred days, the average still puts the main body at ninety percent of its original size.

A plan to use water bombers to spread charcoal dust on the ice surface is scrapped when someone calculates how insignificant an area that would cover.

Similar suggestions to carpet bomb the Fragment with conventional munitions only win favour with those who would profit by supplying the bombs. World War II buffs talk about the days of thousand-bomber raids on Germany, but the time of the big strategic bomber fleet is over. America has only seventy-six B-52s left in service. So that idea too is shelved.

Norman Butchart allows a few cranky hawks to suggest nuking the thing, just to stir up a bit of international protest and give the opposition something to focus their bile on.

The handover of the Fragment from the South Equatorial Current to the Caribbean Current is remarkably clean. A few hundred outlying icebergs are split off by Brazil's shoulder and take the southern route, down the eastern coast of South America, as the EFC's chairman had hoped the whole Fragment would.

But the main body, still containing the four fortresses of ancient glacial ice from the Byrd, Nimrod, Beardmore, and Shackleton Glaciers, skirts the Doldrums and moves north, past the mouth of the Amazon, where the two freshwater giants exchange liquid greetings.

The Fragment's presence has one positive effect. Throughout February the weather in the West Indies has been remarkably tame. A tropical storm's power is driven by heated, rising air. But the Fragment's towering cloud cover has stalled that process. For hundreds of miles beyond its white perimeter, caught in an uncanny balance, the tropical atmosphere is close to static. Without wind the seas are eerily flat and calm. Nothing stirs the palm trees.

Now in the Fragment's path lies the archipelago known as the Windward Islands. The ice shelf neatly slides into the broad gap between the western outliers of Barbados to the north and Tobago to the south, but it will not miss the holiday destinations of Grenada, Saint Vincent and the Grenadines.

They stand before the Fragment like a Civil War picket line against an oncoming army. The tourists are long gone. The residents with money or government connections or even a boat have fled. But the poor and dispossessed have been left behind. And the exodus has decapitated their governments.

In the face of such utter destruction, these governments are bankrupt. Among the poorest nations in the world, they haven't the money, and cannot obtain the credit to save themselves.

And what of the great naval powers? Similar conversations play out in cabinet rooms around the world.

"If we take those people onto our ships, they belong to us."

"We can't do it."

In the final days, the International Red Cross and Red Crescent step forward, offering lucrative contracts to charter any ship they can find to ferry the refugees. They approach all of the cruise lines, including the White Star Line. All decline. With no country prepared to accept the refugees, their insurance companies will not brook the risk of taking on stateless passengers. White Star VP of Marketing, Forest Langford is not available for comment.

The people on the shore are defenseless. Seventy-five thousand on Grenada. Seventy thousand on Saint Vincent and the Grenadines.

Then, across the waters, like a memory of Dunkirk, the small boats come. Fishing boats from the poorest villages of Dominica, Guadeloupe and Martinique. Motor yachts and sailing ketches from the rich marinas of Antigua and Saint Lucia. Working tugs from ports of call around the region. Small boats of every size and quality; in groups, or pairs, or alone. Among them is a sloop whose stern bears the name of *Marcy V.*

At Dunkirk over three hundred thousand soldiers were rescued over the course of nine days, with the little boats crossing and re-crossing the narrow English Channel, amid the bombs and bullets, at distances of forty or fifty miles for each trip.

But, unlike the German Army's advance into Belgium, there will be no Halt Order for the Fragment.

Tearful parents entrust their children to utter strangers and each little boat takes on dozens of these precious passengers, many to the level of recklessness, and then go to find a safe haven to unload. For those leaving Saint Vincent, the closest land is Saint Lucia, twenty miles to the north. For those taken from Grenada, the nearest landfall is a hundred miles to the south.

The Fragment makes its presence known while the small boats arrive and gather their cargo. The fog that precedes it is a dripping thing, an apparition that rises like smoke from land and sea. Thick and white, it blinds. Many of the little boats have no radar and no one knows if they will be able to find their way out of the chaos of hidden reefs and sandbars. But all, even the poorest vessel, has a radio, and through those radios comes a call, as loud and as clear as a highland rallying cry.

"This is Blair Cockburn, master of the *Marcy V.* Don't be afraid. Look to the waters. I've called them. The whales are coming. The whales are coming to guide you."

In English, Spanish, and Portuguese, Cockburn repeats his message.

Among the small-boat crews many have heard of this wonder, the discovery of the Maori scientist, Graham Palmer. And they cast their bread upon the waters.

Once the boats reach water deep enough to support the great creatures, dozens, scores of whales find them.

The whales have come from across who knows how many leagues to risk their lives, to face this danger. Fins and greys have come. Right whales and humpbacks too. And one brave pod of blues; Ring's pod, his father, Milk-Eye, and all the rest, who have been following the Fragment these long months. They come to guide the blind boats, the blind men, through the impenetrable fog.

Sixty-five thousand souls still line the shores of Grenada. Another fifty thousand remain on Saint Vincent and the Grenadines. Many now flee inland, to higher ground, following the few roads that penetrate the interior. The roads are rough and narrow. The islands' best lie close to the sea, the better to serve the tourist trade. The people left behind on the shore are defenceless when the ice comes. At McMurdo, at Scott Base, and at Stanley, you could at least see it coming. On Grenada, Saint Vincent and the Grenadines vision is lost, confounded. The fog swirls like a hallucination before their eyes. And there is the absence of the sound of the surf. So much a part of island life; not to hear the surf is to believe you've gone deaf or mad. The Fragment has stifled the wind, and cut the reach between its face and the shoreline to nothing.

Fire and Ice

The people are defenceless. But in a sense, the islands themselves are not.

In the hurried discussions about what the Fragment might do, and what to do about it, few have considered the topography and geology of these islands.

The Windward Islands are volcanic in origin and are home to a surprisingly large number of active volcanoes, including *La Soufrière* (The Sulfurer) on Saint Vincent, and the submarine volcano, Kick 'em Jenny, some six miles north of Grenada.

The Jenny's crown lies a few hundred feet below the Caribbean's surface, in constant battle with the ocean for supremacy. Liquid rock against liquid water, releasing fumaroles of steam and noxious vapours, constantly boiling the seawater that passes overhead.

The Fragment finds and amputates the Jenny's crown. The upper five hundred metres of the volcanic cone is sheared away and plunges down the slope into the Grenada Basin, 3000 metres below. The displaced cap-rock sheds tidal waves west. In two hours they reach the shores of Jamaica. In four hours the low-lying Yucatan Peninsula. Cancun is awash.

But that is not the worst of it. With a conic section cut away, thousands of square metres of molten lava encounter the moving underside of the frozen giant. Ice and water are flashed to steam. Trapped under the overburden of oncoming ice, the pressure builds. Pushed beyond a superheated state, the molecules of water are rent into their constituent parts, hydrogen and oxygen, a dangerous combination to place in the presence of heat, and heat is something Jenny has plenty of.

The pressurized plasma of H and O explodes upward, channeled by the surrounding ice, the Fragment providing both fuel and combustion chamber for the violence. Like a million Atlas rocket engines facing the wrong way, the plume blasts upward through the atmosphere, a jet of gas and rock, a column of light half a mile wide and brighter than the sun.

The surrounding atmosphere that has been so precariously balanced releases weeks of stored potential and lightning strikes bloom outward.

Islanders who followed the EFC's advice and took refuge on the high ground are the first to perish.

The Grenadines, tiny islands, are struck by sheets, waves of lightning. Every living thing is flashed to vapour, the ground melted and re-melted to glass.

On Saint Vincent, the high caldera of *La Soufrière* is a natural lightning rod and draws its share of attention. Its outer shell is riven and pyroclastic clouds flow down into the tropical forests, rushing to meet the oncoming ice at the shore.

The fortress of ancient glacial ice that was once part of the Shackleton Glacier reaches the Jenny's furnace and these twin colossi contend for possession of the planet.

The upper cone of the Jenny is stripped again, deeper, by the glacial ice, and the out-gassing rocket redoubles. Around the globe, seismographs that have already registered world-shaking compression waves go red-line, and GPS systems start to crash as the planet itself moves a fraction of a metre within its orbit.

Lava bombs fly upward. Some reach sub-orbital velocity and the International Space Station goes dark. The globe spins west and the dust cloud spreads. The strong West African sun fades to moonshine. In New York, Tokyo, and elsewhere the price of grain skyrockets and the stock market dissolves under an avalanche of sell orders. Midwest farmers padlock granaries and Russian oligarchs call out the troops.

In the Maelstrom

Blair Cockburn finds that after a single run most of the whales and humans are satisfied with having faced death once and survived. They choose not to make another attempt.

But a few, the braver or more foolhardy, undertake a second rescue mission.

An old blue signals to him that there are still boats out there, laden with child refugees, lost in the fog.

To Cockburn it seems as if the old whale wants to redeem himself for some earlier failure. And as an old salt himself, with a lot of mistakes under his belt, he finds it impossible to admit to fear in the face of this courage.

So it comes to be that, alone on the *Marcy*, guided by an enormous barnacled blue whale with one milky eye, he is among the few to assay a second attempt.

When the ash-fall starts the Scotsman insists they turn back and he directs his new friend to take what refuge he can under the boat's hull. For a time the *Marcy* is able to offer a sheltering roof to the whale.

But the ash covers and clings to the little boat's deck. The inches quickly grow, and Cockburn can do nothing to stop the roll. The *Marcy* is swamped and he is in the water.

The whale rises, holding him up out of the sea, just as he had seen Ring do for Kate, refusing to dive out of the pelting rain of pumice.

The man places himself on hands and knees over the blowholes, to shelter the whale from the falling ash as best he can.

When the end comes they are cemented together.

As one, a strange conjoined beast, they fall away into the depths.

The Fragment

The Fragment is broken.

Jenny and *La Soufrière* have split the ice shelf. It bears massive, gaping wounds. Shackleton's fortress is a ruin.

The Fragment is broken, but three enormous glacial remnants escape the Windward Island carnage. Each is a score of miles wide and half again that in length. Their upper surfaces are now armoured and encrusted in metres of ash. The Caribbean Current sweeps the Byrd, Nimrod, and Beardmore black ice fortresses onward.

In the chaos they pass west and then north, through the Yucatan Channel, between the wrecked beaches of Cancun and the western tip of Cuba, into the Gulf of Mexico.

The Gulf Coast

The oil men of the American Gulf Coast are romantics. Their offshore wells boast names like Mars, Europa and Genesis, many of which produce oil at the astonishing rate of 37,000 barrels a day.

Remembering the BP Deepwater Horizon disaster, the president orders the hundreds of offshore rigs, from Texas to Alabama, to be shut down and plugged.

In 2010 the Deepwater Horizon gushed for eighty-seven days and an estimated 4.9 million barrels were discharged. After several failed efforts to contain the flow, the well was declared sealed and BP settled with the government for $42 billion in damages.

Byrd is the first ice fortress to find a deepwater rig. A billion dollars in concrete and steel is easily crumpled and soon dozens more fall to Byrd and his brothers.

Thankfully the cement plugs for these deep wells, thousands of feet below the ocean's surface, remain untouched.

But that is not so for many hundreds of the shallow-water wells. The three glacial fortresses peel layers of sediment away from the bedrock of shale. Newly anchored in rock that has been weakened by drilling and fracking, these plugs cannot hold. By the score they rupture and blow, spewing uncounted millions of barrels of crude into the Gulf.

The oil buoys the fortresses up and lubricates their passages farther up onto the fragile continental shelf.

When viewed from space the southern coast of America resembles a lace curtain. From South Padre Island, up past Corpus Christi and New Orleans, to the panhandle of Florida, much of the coastline can only be described as impermanent. At random points a slowly rotating fortress glances off the margins. Barrier islands are torn, swept up and re-deposited like so many coffee grounds.

And now the fortresses find the Mississippi Delta. Which glacial fragment is which has been lost in their twirling, rotating passage, but one catches Raccoon Point and the other two pile in behind it, a reunion of Antarctic cousins. The land is soft, almost liquid, a sampling of American detritus: the silt of every state from Minnesota to Louisiana liberally mixed with trash.

The Big Muddy, from its headwaters at Lake Itasca, Minnesota, where the Civilian Conservation Corps once created man-made rock rapids to entertain summer tourists, confronts scores of dams and locks, shaping its flow, on its way to the Delta. The Upper Mississippi alone has 321 roller gates and tainter gates, but none was ever designed to stop the river. At each, as planned, the water over-tops the dam, or flows through spillways.

Abraham Lincoln knew that to break the South you must take control of the Mississippi River.

But it's not the Fragment that plugs the Mississippi. The river is plugged by the mountain of silt, clay, rocks, and trees, and the smashed buildings and bridges that it pushes before it.

The fortresses jostle to push this new moraine into place, like a cork in a bottle.

Now the low pressure system caused by the Fragment's cold reaches out to the cold fronts of the north — the so-called Polar Vortex — and rain, seeded by Jenny's stratospheric volcanic dust particles, surpasses the level of the Great Flood of 1937. Rain storms lash the continent as never before. The Old Muddy's flow of over 3,000,000 cubic feet per second doubles to 6,000,000.

From basins reaching Alberta to the north, Denver to the west, and Pittsburgh to the east, the flood comes. The Arkansas, the Illinois, the Missouri, the Ohio, the Tennessee, the Cumberland, the Red of the South, all feed the Mississippi. All overtop their banks. The flooding is Biblical. Millions are left homeless. Tens of thousands die.

The Old Man lashes at the moraine's restraint. It seeks, as it has so often in the past, a new channel, and a weak spot is found at Alexandria on the Red and whole towns disappear. The waters break through and open a new mouth one-hundred-and-fifty miles to the west.

Through spring the waters drain. A few remaining pieces of the Fragment that were trapped in the mud are caught in the flow and carried out to sea.

For a few more weeks, like boogie-men, they appear now and again to frighten, but none is large enough to catch the currents and rise up out of the sea.

The Fragment's life is over.

"Oil spills are job creators"

Six weeks after the Gulf disaster the old Washington regime falls in a flurry of resignations, mental breakdowns, and impeachments.

The interim government seeks answers and the reports are not good.

In the Gulf, much of the emergency infrastructure has been swept away. Allies and even former enemies are willing to send whatever emergency personnel, vehicles, and supplies they have, but no one has prepared for this.

Hundreds of the Gulf Coast oil wells will gush until they are empty.

Or they would, if not for a new world community.

The nation of whales steps up again. Fitted with modified air tanks, they guide capping pylons into place. Many die from the pollution and the dangerous, rushed operations.

With the help of Graham and a team of Maori negotiators, Ring demands huge fees, enough money to give the whales a place at the international bargaining table.

As a side-bar, all criminal charges against Clint Rymill, Hank Skelton, and the three scientists are dropped.

One Decade Later

It's a very different world, but there are still television networks, and more people in more countries than ever before want to see today's ceremony in Oslo, Norway.

After the initial interviews with Jay and Nancy back on the *Rose Sayer*, Graham Palmer had hoped to stay out of the limelight and get back to work. But he soon realized that everyone needed to hear about Ring and the many peoples of the sea.

Oh yes, the sea is full of people.

In the months following Graham's breakthrough, scientists the world over had made other first contacts. Other Kiwis were the first to talk with the finback whales. Oh, how Graham envies them that. And the fins — the aquatic kind, not Norway's close neighbours — are proud of having been the inspiration for Graham — as they put it, "the man who taught the humans how to speak."

Meanwhile the Finns — the Scandinavian kind, not the whales — have adopted their name-brothers and threaten a Winter War on any nation that conducts whaling of any kind, not mentioning the Norwegians by name.

A team in California followed up with the humpback whale breakthrough.

The Americans got quite an earful from that species. As one of the few whales that mate and give birth in shallow coastal lagoons, the humpbacks had long been fed up with nosy researchers with underwater cameras snooping around during times that should be respected as private.

The humpbacks announced: Any researcher willing to fornicate and give birth in public is welcome to come and watch us do the same. Everyone else should get the hell out of the lagoons.

The Dutch, pursuing work done in the Indian Ocean during the 1970s, reintroduced themselves to the sperm whales, and the enthusiasm of the Dutch public for learning sperm whale symbols has become second to none.

A Canadian team had contacted the last few hundred grey whales, but that was an unsettling conversation. The greys said they didn't want their calves wandering the seas alone, so, with so few left, they had decided to stop procreating and just let nature take its course. They know they will be the last generation of their kind to swim the ocean world.

The Canadians called in grief counselors from across the world. Only time will tell if that will make any difference.

And the myriad species of whale have learned to talk not only *to* humans, but *through* human translators, *to each other.* Blues and finbacks, like long lost cousins, have spent years comparing notes and learning each other's history.

The orcas have gotten an earful (and not a few threats) from all their cousins about the eating of fellow whales. Always the sharp ones, they immediately apologized for past sins and began organizing along democratic lines. Several bulls have started to campaign for elected office.

Cultures are shared and new ideas are fertilized. Sperm whales laugh at a translation of *Moby Dick*, puzzle over the Bible's Jonah, and complain about Disney's *Pinocchio.*

Composers, whale and human, collaborate in a new Renaissance of world music.

Today is the culmination of a long process: the successful application, led by aboriginal peoples in Canada and the Maoris of New Zealand, for the UN to admit a new nation for membership: the Nation of Whales, claiming ownership of everything outside the 200 mile coastal limits.

Graham stands at the podium. He turns for a moment to study the stunning murals of the Oslo City Hall behind him. In the front row, amid the dignitaries, is his deaf father, proud in a rented tuxedo.

Eric and Kate flank his Dad. Next to Kate are Clint Rymill and their little one, a sweet four-year-old girl named Lily, after Clint's mother. Then come Mafri, Hank Skelton, and other members of the *Lincoln*'s whale study crew, all civilians now, along with Jay and Al.

A seat has been left empty to honour their lost, brave friend, Blair Cockburn.

The hall hushes.

"We all know the human tragedies that the Fragment has visited upon the world." Graham speaks to the audience, and to the cameras that will carry him to a billion screens around the globe. "Stanley. The Caribbean. The American Gulf Coast."

He pauses. "Memories of these events will fade, but one fact will not. For all of history, the human race has been in solitary confinement. And as a person alone loses perspective, so too has our entire species lost perspective."

He signals his friends, Eric, Kate, Rymill, and the rest, to join him on the stage.

He smiles at each of them as they file up, then turns back to the audience. "This is our chance to stop being crazy. There are other intelligent beings on Planet Earth. We finally have someone to talk to — and the conversation is just beginning."

His dad signs to him, "Do you wish to know me?" and he sees Kate and Rymill's little girl watching the older man's eloquent hands, her own tiny fingers unconsciously forming the same words. Kate sees it too and whispers in her husband's ear. They both look like they've had more practice smiling.

Graham continues. "We've all paid a heavy price for our arrogance and greed. But new leaders are showing us a better way. New human leaders. New whale leaders. Time will tell if we all have the courage of our convictions.

"Thank you. Thanks, all. Now please welcome my friend and teacher, Ring, the world's first President of Whales."

Behind them, a blank projection screen drops from the ceiling. Ring's rumbling voice plays through speakers, the house lights dim and whale symbols appear.

It is time to sing again.